The Trade - Off

- Creating A Life Worth Living -

Tim Connor

Tim Connor

"A man's mind plans his way, but the Lord directs his steps."

Proverbs 16:9

The Trade - Off

-Creating A Life Worth Living-

Copyright: 1999 Tim Connor

Library of Congress Catalogue No: In Publication

All rights reserved under International and Pan American Copyright Conventions including reproductions in whole or in part in any form.

ISBN: 1-930376-00-6

Published by: Connor Resource Group

Cover Design: George Foster

Editor: Kristin Boykin

Manufactured in: The United States of America

First Printing: December 1999

For information on Tim's services as a meeting or convention speaker please call: 800-222-9070 or 800-222-9071 (fax)
E-Mail; speaker@bellsouth.net.

Tim Connor

Books by Tim Connor

Soft Sell

The Voyage

The Mission

Crossroads

Sales Mastery

The Ancient Scrolls

Daily Success Journal

Win-Win Selling

The Road to Happiness

The Road to Happiness Fun-Book

Walk Easy with Me Through Life

*Let's Get Back to Basics
Personal Development Series*

The Trade - Off

"The future just didn't happen, it was created."

Will Durant

Tim Connor

- Dedication -

To

Charlie "Tremendous" Jones

My friend, mentor, hero and inspiration.

"In life there are choices, decisions and actions and, in the end, each of them has a consequence. Some end in positive outcomes while others end in negative ones, but you cannot escape them."

Tim Connor

Or to quote the popular phrase…

'What goes around – comes around.'

- Prologue -

Jason pleaded with his well-conditioned legs to carry him just a hundred more yards. He knew the terrain, so he was able to look back over his shoulder every few seconds to see if he was gaining on him. Sweat was pouring off his face. His shirt and shorts were soaked with the sweat of several hundred yards of nonstop sprinting. He was operating now on pure adrenaline. Although he was the state champion in the one hundred-yard dash for the past four years, he never had to run for his safety in his dozens of races. He ran because he loved to run. Now, he was running for his life.

He was gaining on him. Just forty more yards to safety. Would Jason make it this time? Thirty, twenty, ten. He was now within arms reach. Five... Jason could feel his ugly breath on his neck, like the hot summer wind.

The Trade - Off

"I made it." And then he collapsed.

Jason could hear the soft, gentle voice call to him as if it were a million miles away.

"Jason! Jason, wake up, it is time to get ready for school."
"Mom, is that you?"
"Yes, son. Who were you expecting?"

The dream was as fresh in his mind as if he had actually lived through the chase just moments earlier. This was a recurring dream for him. And yet each time there was something different about the dream. He couldn't quite put his finger on it, but he knew that one night soon, he would not make it to safety.

"Good morning Mom. I had that dream again."
Jason suddenly realized that his T-shirt was soaking wet, and he was exhausted - as tired as if he had just run three successive qualifying trials in the same morning.

"Jason, why don't you see that doctor who I mentioned last week?"

"Mom, I am not going to see a shrink. What if my friends found out? I would be the laughingstock of the whole school. And I am only a few days away from graduation. I will consider it this summer."

"OK, but I believe Dr. Cohen can really help you."

"Mom, I have to handle this myself, in my own way. OK?"

"I understand. Please get dressed and come down for breakfast."

Jason's mom closed the door behind her and left him with the silence of his own thoughts. He lay there for a few minutes trying to make some sense out of his dream. Little did he know how the choices and decisions he made for the first third of his life would impact his happiness, lifestyle, relationships and success from that point on.

The date was May 15th.

The Trade - Off

"The great end in life is not knowledge, but action."

Thomas Huxley

- Chapter One -

It always started the same. Jason was getting ready to leave work. He had been working several years for the company, and had earned a reputation as one of the bright new stars of Bellvedere Industries. His most recent promotion came just weeks ago. Now the head of the sales and marketing group for this four hundred million dollar-a-year business, he hadn't yet reached his thirtieth birthday. He was the youngest person ever to hold this position in the history of the company. He was not over his head, but he had to work longer hours, and six and often seven-day weeks to keep ahead of the president's expectations of him.

Jason did everything with a sense of urgency and focus. He never undertook any goal, activity or project lightly because he felt that to do so was to cheat the outcome.

The Trade - Off

He could have been a Hollywood actor. He was trim, and his 5'10" frame was the envy of many professional athletes. He had a rugged handsomeness, and his emerald green eyes sparkled with a brightness that was a perfect companion to his glowing smile. Jason was the first person in his high school's history to be selected as both *Most Likely to Succeed* and *Best Looking*. These accolades, however, never went to his head. He believed that his looks were the gift of his genes and that his will to succeed would be tested again and again in the real world, regardless of the opinions of his classmates.

He loved his job, the company, and the freedom he was given, but the responsibilities took a heavy toll on his personal and family life. His wife was constantly nagging him to spend more time with her. She complained that he was a stranger to his two children.

As Jason lay in his bed half teased by the drift in and out of consciousness, he looked around his room filled with trophies, ribbons and all of the trappings of victory and success, and he was still only eighteen.

Tim Connor

His mind drifted back to the dream.

He felt under increasing pressure to leave work earlier, and yet he felt the need to work just a few more hours each day. He knew he was sacrificing the relationship with his family, but he was doing it for them. The house, cars, vacations and all of the trappings of success required him to keep climbing the corporate ladder - higher and higher, year after year.

The face of the person chasing him in the dream had not yet been revealed, and he didn't know why he was being chased. He only knew that, for some strange reason, he felt compelled to run from him. Maybe next time when the dream occurs, he will – once and for all - stop and confront his assailant.

"Jason, your breakfast is ready."

"Coming, mom."

On his way to school, Jason thought about how he was going to spend his summer. He had three months of freedom before he had to be on the campus of his new home for the next four years. He looked

The Trade - Off

forward to this time of his life with both fear and positive anticipation. Fear that he would not be able to live up to the expectations of so many people, including himself, and the excitement of beginning a new phase of his life.

Jason was a responsible teen. He was looked up to by many of his classmates for his maturity, fun-loving spirit and dedication to whatever he set his mind to do. As he entered the front door of the high school, one of his best friends, Marjorie, stopped him in his tracks when she screamed, "I made it! I was accepted at Harvard!" She leaped at Jason and gave him the biggest hug he thought possible.

"Congratulations, Kiddo. I knew all along you would make it. Is Harvard ready for you?"

"I promise you, Jason Conroy, I will make my mark in that school before I am finished. They will never forget Marjorie Adkins."

Tim Connor

Marjorie and Jason shared their first class, so they walked together down the long busy corridor discussing their plans for the summer. They had been friends since grade school and were destined to remain friends - although at a distance - except for an unexpected turn of events that neither could have ever foreseen.

As the day moved on Jason kept coming back to his dream and its meaning. Was there some message in it that he was failing to see? He decided after school to visit the library and find a book on the interpretation of dreams to see if it could shed some light on the cause of his recurring drama.

After a few hours of research, he discovered what he believed was the dream's purpose. It was unfortunate that his interpretation was based on a limited understanding of how the unconscious mind works and that he wasn't even close to what it was trying to tell him about his unknown future. Relieved, thinking that he understood, he returned the book, put the dream out of his mind, and headed home. It was a busy night filled with family discussions about his plans for

The Trade - Off

the summer and with his younger brother's unhappy acceptance of attending summer school again this year. Jimmy was not as dedicated a student as Jason, so he struggled with the routines of attending school and homework. The family talked well into the evening - a rare event - until Jason announced that he was tired and going to bed.

He fell off to sleep easily, and once more found himself in the midst of the dream. The scenes, sounds and faces were very familiar to him now. They were like old friends, if only make-believe ones.

"Jason," Cinamon called, "dinner is ready."

Jason left his study in turmoil. He had hours of work to do and would have preferred to skip dinner and try to make some headway into the piles of reports, product reviews, personnel files, and various papers that needed his immediate attention. Something inside, however, told him he better not disappoint Cin and his two children, Jeffrey and Cindy.

Tim Connor

Both the children had benefited from the good looks of their mother - who was a radiant beauty. Her long auburn hair, deep blue eyes and perfect smile rounded out what Jason believed was the most beautiful woman he had ever seen. He often felt inadequate in her presence, which was a strain between them in what otherwise he thought was a perfect relationship. Her name was Cinamon, but he liked to call her Cin because it reminded him of her playful spirit and the sensual and graceful way she carried her 5'6" and 120 pounds. They were deeply in love and had been from the moment they met in their first year in college. They had met by chance at a fraternity party that neither had planned to attend. At the urging of friends, they both showed up at the same time and introduced themselves to each other on the front steps of the building.

There was a spark - a special connection - that they both instantly felt. From that moment on there was never any doubt that they would spend the rest of their lives together. It was a storybook

The Trade - Off

meeting - one that amazed their friends. All through college, neither had the slightest interest or curiosity in dating anyone else.

Their love was passionate, sweet and adoring. The children arrived within the first two years of marriage and only deepened their love for each other as they watched them begin to take on the unique blend of their personalities and looks.

"Coming Cin," Jason yelled upstairs from his office. When he arrived in the dining room there were candles and a birthday cake on the sideboard.

"Who is the cake for?" he asked.

With that simple remark, Cindy went crying out of the room and Cinamon gave Jason the biggest scowl he had ever seen.

"You have been so wrapped up in yourself that you are not even aware that it is your daughter's 5th birthday. Jason, enough is enough! This is the last straw! Either you come back to Earth and become an active member of this family, or we are leaving and you can work 24 hours a day and none of us will care."

This jolted Jason into reality. He had never realized the demands of his job and his schedule had come to this point. He broke down and tears flooded from his eyes.

"I am so sorry. I have been working these incredible hours these past months for you and the kids. I have wanted you all to have what so often I missed as a child."

"Jason, the most important thing you missed as a child was adequate time with your family. And, you are re-creating the drama with our children without even knowing it. We would much rather have you than all of this stuff you seem to think is so important to us. There are trade-offs in life, Jason. You make one decision and you get one set of consequences, make another decision and you get an entire new set of outcomes or actions. Life, my dear, is about

The Trade - Off

decisions and consequences, and you are trading off some of the most important parts of your life for things that don't really matter. I beg you to rethink your motives and actions before it is too late for all of us."

Tim Connor

"If you do not expect the unexpected, you will not find it."

Heraclitus

- Chapter Two -

The morning began like every other for Jason. A quick breakfast by himself in the semi darkness of the comfortable eat-in kitchen. Their home was a sprawling ranch tucked neatly on three acres without any other homes in view. While he played with his cereal, he thought about the many decisions that required his careful attention later that day.

The children were still tucked in their beds, waiting for the sun to peak over the horizon. Cin was in the bathroom taking a leisurely bath while listening to soft music and contemplating her life and the day before her.

Cinamon was a committed mother, and yet she still found ample time for her career as a social counselor for the less fortunate. Although she had known relative affluence since she and Jason had begun their married life together, she still stayed close to her belief that there were people who, despite their early conditions and adversities, deserved support, guidance and someone who cared about them and their circumstances.

Jason finished his breakfast and said good-bye to his wife and left for work before most people even thought about what the day might bring.

On his way to work, Jason called his boss, Frank Crandall, from his car and confirmed their seven AM meeting with the VP of finance Bert Saunders. Frank although only forty-five years old, was considered one of the brightest business owners in the rapidly growing computer industry. He had started the firm in his garage when he was in his early twenties, and within five years had built the company to over 400 employees and eighty million in annual sales. He had met Jason at a computer trade show while he was a sales rep for a competitor. They resonated immediately and within three months Jason was hired as a sales rep for national accounts. It

The Trade - Off

was one of the best hiring decisions that Frank had made, and he was secretly grooming Jason to become president of the firm. He had not given Jason any clues, however. He didn't want to prejudice his performance. Frank had other more visionary designs and wanted within five years to begin one of his pet projects, a new computer process that would revolutionize the industry beyond anyone's wildest imagination. It was Frank's personal agenda to keep the technology secret until he could devote his full time to the development of the idea. He needed Jason to learn as much as he could as quickly as possible. Time was running out for Frank. There were several other major players in the computer industry that could upstage him at any moment.

Bert Saunders was your basic bean counter. Good at what he did, but restricted by structure, policy and what could be demonstrated on paper. One of Jason's greatest strengths was his ability to think out of the box. This morning's meeting was to discuss the budget and details for an expansion plan to build new plants in four different countries: Argentina, Japan, Africa and China. There were tremendous challenges in this expansion in the financial, political and logistical areas. Whoever headed up the project would have to spend months traveling internationally to get each operation up and running within two to three years.

Frank hadn't shared his plan with either Bert or Jason. This was the purpose of this morning's meeting as well as brainstorming potential opportunities and difficulties. He knew Jason would buy into the plan, but he wasn't sure about Bert. He needed Jason to help sway Bert in his direction. Even though Bert was an excellent executive, he acted as if he were spending his own money - a trait that both frustrated and reassured Frank.

Jason was first to arrive for the early meeting. He waited patiently in the conference room for Frank and Bert to arrive, wondering about the purpose of this early morning meeting. Frank had told him to leave the entire morning open. This was an unusual request. Franks' meetings usually never lasted more than thirty minutes. He got to the point, asked for input, made decisions and then adjourned his

The Trade - Off

meetings abruptly. While Jason waited, he was brought back to Cin's remark the other night about becoming an active member of the family before it was too late. He needed to discuss with Frank his need to cut back on his hours and responsibilities. His career was important to him. He liked the income and responsibility, but his relationships with Cin and the children were now more important to him than his job.

Jason was one of the most talented sales executives in the country. He could easily find another position with a smaller firm. Although he might not be able to bring home the four hundred thousand dollars a year, at least he would have some free time for himself and his family. Frank was a driven business owner and recently his demands on Jason had increased to the breaking point. Jason was totally unaware of Frank's plans for him.

"Good Morning Jason. Have you seen Bert yet this morning?'

"No, but I am sure he will be here shortly. It's still only six forty-five."

"Good. This will give us a few minutes to talk before he arrives. Let's grab a cup of coffee in my office."

Jason followed Frank to his office, wondering why they couldn't just talk in the conference room. When they arrived, Frank unveiled a large glass display on his solid cherry 12-foot conference table. The display showed several large buildings spaced evenly with parking garages, landscaping and interconnecting highways. It was a sprawling network of architectural splendor, with modern buildings constructed of unique glass and stonework.

"What's all this Frank?"

"Our expansion plans for growth for the next five years."

"Where are these buildings?"

"Argentina, Japan, Africa and China. What do you think?"

"Seems like an aggressive undertaking. Who is going to be responsible for overseeing this program?"

The Trade - Off

"Jason, I would like you to take on this assignment. What do you think? It would mean a significant increase in your salary as well as the opportunity of a lifetime!"

Jason didn't hear Frank's last sentence. He was wrapped up in his own thoughts about Cin and what this would mean to their marriage. This could be the final straw in a relationship that Jason had recently discovered was beginning to unravel.

"Frank, I will have to think about it. I need some time and I need to discuss it with my wife. I have already been accused recently of playing absentee husband and father. This needs some gestation time."

"Sorry Jason, you don't have any time. I want this project to begin immediately. I need your decision this morning. I know I am asking a great deal, but please keep in mind I am also turning a 600 million-dollar project over to you with full decision-making capabilities. Our meeting with Bert is to discuss the financial projections and estimate our cash flow, loan ability and projected completion time. Bert spent several years as the controller for a major construction company and his insight will be invaluable in this discussion."

From deep inside Jason felt a nagging sensation that he couldn't place. It was as if a burning ember was slowly increasing its intensity and would soon explode into a full-blown blaze. He felt that he was about to make one of the biggest decisions in his life and he didn't want to make a mistake. His mind raced back and forth weighing all of the possible outcomes if he took on the challenge as well as all of the potential uncertainties in his career and security at Belvedere if he turned Frank down. He liked his job, he loved the company, and he enjoyed working for Frank - even though he was often a driven taskmaster. What would Cin want him to do? The only thing he could think of to slow down the process and find some way to stall was to ask Frank a question.

"Frank, what difference will one day make? I can't believe you would expect me to make this kind of a decision and commitment without talking with Cinamon. She has a right to make her feelings and wishes known and to be a part of this decision. Obviously I would be spending a great deal of time out of the country away from her and the kids. Frank, I need 24 hours!"

"No Jason. I need executives who can make quick and rational decisions."

"But I don't have enough information to make a smart decision."

"You have everything you need. I trust you, I want you to take on the project and I know you have the ability to complete it successfully. What more do you need to know?"

"Well Frank, if you need an answer now, the answer is…"

The phone in Frank's office interrupted his answer. "Yes, Bert. We will be a few more minutes. Please wait for us in the conference room. What else is it?"

Frank stood quietly for what seemed like several minutes as he was obviously receiving some unpleasant news. His facial expression changed almost immediately from neutral to extreme anguish as tears began to roll down his cheeks. In all the years Jason had known Frank he had never seen him cry. He was embarrassed and as he turned away he motioned to Frank to see if he wanted him to leave. Frank didn't even see Jason's gesture; he was in another world. When he hung up he said, "Jason we will have to postpone our meeting and this discussion until another time. I have an emergency. I will be gone for a few days. I will let you know when we can reschedule our meeting.

Jason left wondering what in the world could have had such an affect on his boss. Frank was strong, fearsome and seldom showed any emotions whatsoever. This was an entirely new side of Frank. His feelings were curiosity as well as concern for his friend. Before he crossed the threshold, he turned and said, "Is there anything I can do Frank?"

"No, and I'll explain later."

But later would not be for several years. Jason never saw Frank again.

The Trade - Off

Jason wondered many times during the next several years what had happened to Frank. Why he just literally dropped off the face of the Earth, without a trace. The other strange question that always bothered Jason was why that phone message was given to Frank that morning by Bert and not directly to him from the unknown source. There were other questions that nagged at Jason's consciousness but he believed all would be answered some day.

As a consequence of Frank's lengthy absence, Belvedere was sold to a competitor a few months later and the expansion plans were shelved. Jason's new boss was the Vice President of sales for the acquiring company and was a very political and incompetent individual. Jason walked into his office after three weeks and quit. No notice - just like that - he quit. No severance, just emptied his desk and said goodbye. And he never looked back, not once.

Years later, as Jason was working late in his office in the house, his private line rang.

Tim Connor

"Jason, this is Frank. How are you?"

"I am fine, thanks. Where are you? What happened? Why did you drop out of society? Are you OK?"

"Jason, slow down. I will give you the best answers I can, but I don't have much time, so please just listen."

That morning seven years ago, my wife and three daughters were on their way home from visiting my wife's parents. They had been driving most of the night. When they pulled off the highway for gas they were sideswiped by an eighteen wheeler and were thrown off the road into a ditch. The car rolled several times, caught fire and exploded. They were all killed instantly. This was the report filed to the police by a driver who was directly behind them.

Jason, my family was everything to me. I loved them more than my own life. I spent twenty-five years building Belvedere in order to give them everything they wanted and needed to have a secure and happy and peaceful life. I am aware now that all of my sacrifice, the

The Trade - Off

times when I wouldn't see them for several days due to travel or the hundreds of meals I missed with them wasn't worth it. I never really saw my girls grow up. I missed all of the significant events of their life – concerts, soft ball games, everything.

I convinced myself that the sacrifice was worth the trade-off. I missed so much by focusing only on building my business. If I could put the clock in reverse, I would have walked away from Belvedere after several years. I certainly no longer needed the money. I was chasing more, bigger, better and all the trappings of success. My friend, success means nothing if what is really important to you is suddenly taken from you. I was called to the morgue in an attempt to identify the bodies. There was nothing left of the four of them but unrecognizable charred remains. Jason, it was the most horrifying sight I have ever seen.

The trauma and the guilt suddenly got hold of me and I totally lost it. I cleaned out my bank accounts, sold the house, no - I really gave it away, got in the car and headed south. I just kept driving. I was running from myself. And after several weeks of running, I discovered I could no longer hide from me. I ended up in a little town on the coast of southern Mexico. I spent several months there just walking the beach day after day - trying to make sense out of my life. So many decisions that I had made that seemed right at the time now, in retrospect, could have been so much better. If I could only turn the clock back and re-make many of them, knowing what I know now, I would do so. But the clock can't be turned back by any of us. Decisions always have consequences. Choices are made without regard for the other choices we could make. I made lots of poor choices and I now must spend the rest of my life contemplating their outcomes.

I even considered suicide - but it seemed senseless. It wouldn't have brought them back, but it would have ended my daily pain. I am now doing volunteer work here in a small town in Mexico. I am not exactly sure where I will go next and when. I only know that whatever I do and when I do it, for the rest of my life, it will be for the right reasons and not for outcomes driven by my ego or greed.

The Trade - Off

And whatever the outcome of these decisions - I will leave behind no regrets."

"Jason, I am running out of time and there is one other thing I want you to know. I authorized Bert to sell the company. We had been dancing with several firms about a possible acquisition for over a year. I kept that information from you because I didn't want you to lose your focus. One company made an offer and I agreed. Through Bert, the deal was closed in thirty days. I later heard from Bert that you left the company within a month, something about not getting along with your new boss. Well, I can certainly understand. He was a jerk. I met him on a few occasions during meetings to discuss the acquisition and I couldn't have worked for him either. Jason, I think that brings you up to date."

"Not so fast, Frank. I thought we were good friends. Why has it taken you several years to get in touch with me?"

"Frankly, I was too embarrassed. I felt as though I let you down and I was either too immature or too much into my grief and myself these past years to even think about anyone but myself. I owe you an apology and I ask for your forgiveness. I never meant to hurt you, but I was struggling with life and the simple tasks of getting through each day."

"Frank, you don't need my forgiveness. I was just worried about your well being. I even thought you might be dead."

"Jason, I was dead for the better part of the past several years, but I have recently come to grips with my grief, guilt, anger and remorse. With the help of a Mexican Guide, I have joined the living and can tell you that I now realize, more than ever, the relationship between decisions and consequences. Each decision in my life is now made with a totally different perspective. I only wish it hadn't taken the death of the four people I loved the most in the world to learn it. Juan has spent hundreds of hours with me these past few years helping me to clearly see the real purpose and meaning of life. It is now clear to me what I must do.

Goodbye Jason. You won't hear from me again. I wish you well and I wish you peace, happiness and success. If I can give you one

The Trade - Off

little piece of advice in parting, it would be to make every decision in your life carefully. They all matter - no matter how small or insignificant they may seem at the time. All actions have consequences – some positive and some negative. Some consequences are immediate, while others take more time to gestate before their work is done. One other thing, as a token of my appreciation for all you did for me at Belvedere, I have given your name to Juan."

The phone line went dead and Jason was left with an eerie silence and the rhythm of his own heart beating. Jason had many other questions, but he knew they would go unanswered for the rest of his life.

There was one question he would soon have an answer to, however, and that was why Frank gave his name to Juan.

Tim Connor

"The meaning in life is the meaning that you give it."

Matthew Stasior

The Trade - Off

Chapter Three

"Jason, who was that on the phone?"

"Frank Crandall."

"You are kidding!"

"No, Cin. I am serious. After seven years, he finally gave me an explanation of why he disappeared."

He spent the next half-hour sharing with Cinamon what Frank had told him. She listened intently as he came to the part about Juan.

"Why do you think he told Juan about you?"

"I don't know. But somehow, I feel one day I will find out."

"It's late Jason. Let's go to bed. I need to feel close to you tonight."

"Me too."

Tim Connor

They went upstairs and, after their nightly pre-bed ritual, slid under the covers and held each other tightly. They fell off to sleep in each other's arms. Jason had one of the best night's sleep he had had in years. Even though there were unanswered questions, he finally felt like there was some closure on this memory.

After Jason left Belvedere, he decided to go into business for himself as a consultant. He was in great demand. He was bright, intuitive and gave his clients valuable information that contributed to their success. He didn't match his income with Belvedere but he now had one thing that was missing while he worked for Frank. He had freedom. Freedom to spend time with his family, friends and personal interests. He enjoyed working for himself. He still worked long hours and many weekends but he never missed an important family event. His relationship with his wife gradually improved. It was as if his life was almost too good to be true. Jason often felt, however, that someday the other shoe would drop and this wonderful happy fantasy would end. The children needed less and less from their parents and were becoming young adults with active

The Trade - Off

lives of their own. It reminded Jason of that old Harry Chapin song, *Cat's in the Cradle*. Every time he heard it, it would bring tears to his eyes. The truth of the words in that song were often just too much reality for him.

Jason was lucky, or so he believed. His life had been saved when he had left Belvedere. What he didn't realize was that, when he made the decision to go into business for himself, this decision also brought consequences with it.

The next day, while going through the mail, he noticed a letter with a Mexican stamp on it and no return address. He opened it and read the contents with interest and curiosity.

Dear Jason,

Frank Crandall recently gave me your name. He asked me to wait until he had left our small village before I wrote you. Frank believes that I might be of some help to you. The purpose of this letter is to

Tim Connor

invite you to spend some time with me at your earliest convenience. You are welcome to come at any time.

Regards,
Juan

Jason read and re-read the letter over and over again looking for some clue, any clue that would help him understand why he should drop everything and trudge down to Mexico to visit some spiritual leader. The letter sounded like it was from a business associate - not some Shaman or whatever he was. Jason put the letter in a drawer and forgot about it. He went about his business for several weeks and had forgotten about Juan when a second letter from Juan arrived on a Saturday. Jason studied the envelope and found no return address. The postmark was almost three weeks before which meant that Juan had mailed the second letter shortly after the first. He opened the letter and read.

The Trade - Off

Jason,

I urge you to come before it is too late for you!

Juan

There was no telephone number and no address, so Jason had no way of contacting Jaun to determine the cause for urgency. In the first place, this whole situation seemed a bit bizarre. To rush off to Mexico at the urging of some Mexican lunatic woo-woo person that Jason had never met and had no way of finding - other than he knew the name of the small town from the postmark on the letter - seem farfetched at best.

He threw the letter away and went into the house for lunch. Cinamon had made tuna sandwiches and the two of them ate in relative silence. The kids were off on one of their weekend jaunts with friends, and Jason and Cinamon had the house to themselves for the weekend. Finally, Jason broke the silence with, "I got another letter from that crazy in Mexico."

"What did it say?"

"Something to the effect of come now it is urgent."

"That's it?'

"Yep."

"Are you going to go?"

"Are you serious Cin? Why in the world would I want to travel halfway around the world to visit a crazy old man who may not even speak English?"

"Because you trusted and liked Frank and it was he who gave Juan your name. There must have been a reason."

"I am sure there was, but, if it was so important, why didn't Frank tell me why he gave the old man my name?"

"Jason, you know how Frank was. He would often let you figure things out for yourself. It built your confidence and helped you learn to think and reason more accurately."

The Trade - Off

"You are right about that, I had forgotten. I wonder why Frank wants me to see that old man? He said he had worked with him for over two years to help him put his life back together. Does he believe that I am in the same position?"

"He must have had his reasons. And besides, how do you know he is that old. Frank never mentioned his age."

"I wonder what they were?"

"Look Jason, you have a clear schedule next week. I have to be out of town, and the children can stay with friends. Why don't you go?"

"I will consider it if you will give me one good reason."

"You will never know why Frank did what he did until you go."

"Very good Cin! That's why I love you so much; not only are you the sexiest, most beautiful women I have ever known - you are the brightest as well."

"Dangerous combination, don't you think?"

"Yes, that's why I married you. To save the rest of the male race in America."

"Well there is always Mexico."

"What do you mean?"

"Well, I may just come with you to do a little sightseeing. I have always wanted to visit Mexico."

"No way. If I go, I am going alone. Down, get answers and back in no more than three days."

"So you are going?"

"Yes. I'll check on flights leaving this afternoon. I guess I better see if there is a hotel or brothel in that little town."

"If you come back with anything other than wisdom, you can spend the rest of our married life in the guest room, got it?"

"Got it."

Jason was able to confirm a late afternoon flight to Mexico City with a connection to Oaxaca City. He would then rent a car and drive the rest of the way to Puerto Angel. He had no specific plan as to how he would find Jaun or where he would stay. He was unable to locate a hotel in the small village that had rooms available. As he packed, he contemplated this spontaneous decision. He typically liked to have everything carefully planned before he undertook any project or trip.

The Trade - Off

The previous summer he had renovated a small storage shed on the back of his property and the time that it took from start to completion was several weeks. Any contractor could have finished the job in two days. Jason prided himself on his thoroughness - regardless of the task. This trip certainly promised to be an adventure, even though he knew he would be home by the middle of the next week.

Cinamon took him to the airport and, after a long hug and short kiss good-bye, Jason grabbed his overnight bag from the trunk and headed for the gate.

He felt an uneasy sense of foreboding, as if this trip held more in store for him than he could reasonably contemplate. His only solace was Frank's confidence in Juan. Jason hoped it was well founded.

The trip to Mexico City was uneventful. Jason was seated next to a Mexican grandmother who was off to visit her latest grandchild. She spoke very little English, so Jason had ample time to read, think and, yes, even worry. About what he didn't really know. He was not your typical worrier – he either let things go or he took action. He always felt worry was a senseless use of mental time and accomplished nothing in the long run. In the short run, it sabotaged current creativity, productivity and needlessly increased stress.

His layover in Mexico City was frustrating at best. International travel, unless one is a seasoned veteran, can be very stressful. Since Jason did not speak any Spanish, it was difficult for him to effectively communicate his needs and desires. It took him ten minutes to find the men's bathroom and another fifteen minutes to order a diet Pepsi. These simple, yet exasperating, circumstances contributed even more to his concern about the rest of his journey.

The flight to Oaxaca City was a bit scary. The pilot looked like an ancient Spanish War veteran with an oily shirt, unruly mustache and big cigar, which he smoked while he flew the plane. There were only three other passengers besides Jason, and they looked like drug cartel members. The plane landed at a small airport that had no

The Trade - Off

runway lights and a broken-down building that failed to pass for a terminal. He found the only car rental counter which doubled as a bar where, thankfully, the attendant spoke some English. After completing the details on the car rental contract - which took close to thirty minutes, - and getting what Jason thought were good directions to Puerto Angel, he was finally ready to get on his way. It was now close to midnight. The attendant/bartender recommended that he not drive at night. She said, "The highways are not safe after dark. Robberies and a variety of other miscellaneous criminal acts are common. Senor, many bandits roam the streets each night in search of easy victims." He decided to take the young woman's advice, so she volunteered to help him find lodging for the evening. She found a room for him at the Hotel Soraya high on a bluff overlooking the ocean. She said it was a nice hotel, gave him directions and wished him luck. He left the terminal and found his car in the rental parking lot across the street. Now, the real challenge was to begin. Dealing with foreign road signs, a map written in Spanish and no way of knowing what would happen on the way to the hotel, Jason started the car and drove away.

Tim Connor

He found the hotel with less trouble than he anticipated and checked in with little difficulty. The woman was right; this was a charming little spot. As he walked to his room, he thought how Cin would love this little hotel tucked in at the end of a long winding road with a picturesque view of the ocean. , Normally he would have had to wait until dawn to see the view, but there was a full moon that literally bathed the shore and horizon for miles. It was quite a sight.

The next morning, he began the final stage of the journey that would prove to be one of the significant events of his life. He was driving along what appeared to be a major highway that actually was no better than a second class rural road filled with potholes and very poor signage. He began to wonder why he had left on this crazy adventure in the first place. As far as he was concerned, his relationships, career and life in general were all in wonderful shape. Why did he need the counsel of this old Mexican at this point in his life?

The Trade - Off

He would soon learn, even though his past was in good order by average standards, that the consequences of many of his early life decisions, choices and actions were about to take their toll on the rest of his life.

Jason arrived in the small coastal port of Puerto Angel shortly after lunch. The sun was bright in the middle of a deep blue sky. The town looked deserted as he drove down what seemed to be the main street. He later discovered it was the only street. There were no hotels, two small cafes and what looked like a small general store. Most of the cars were small compacts that had all seen better days.

Why am I here? This is lunacy! Too late… I may as well finish this and leave first thing in the morning - and get back to my normal life.

He entered the general store and asked the only person there where he might find Juan.

The person behind the counter said in broken English,

"I will be glad to help you, Senor. Can you tell me - which Juan? There are 12 Juans in this village and a new one may be on the way. Senora Veronica is delivering her fourth child today and her first three children were boys. If this one is a boy she has said she will call him Juan."

"That is the best I can do. I don't know his last name."

"Can you tell me a little about him? - A description, where he works, where he lives?"

Jason suddenly realized he had traveled half way around the world looking for one person in a secluded village knowing nothing about him. He said, half to himself and half out loud, "Is this crazy or what?"

"Pardon, Senor?"

"He is a spiritual advisor of some kind. That is all I can tell you."

The attendant gave Jason a strange look as if this gringo wasn't quite all there.

The Trade - Off

"That helps a little, Senor. I believe you are looking for Juan Lopez. He lives a few miles just outside of town in a small pink adobe house."

"Can you give me directions?"

"Just drive to the end of the main street and turn left at your first road. There is a vacant old post office on the corner. From there it is about 2 miles on the left. You can't miss it."

"Thank you for your help."

"By the way, Juan is not there today."

"Where can I find him?"

"He has gone to a yearly retreat in a small town about thirty miles from here."

"Do you know when he will return?"

"He is usually gone for several days when he attends these gatherings."

"Do you know the name of the town?"

"Well, it really isn't a town like this one, my friend - just a piece of land between here and nowhere."

Tim Connor

"Does it have a name?"

"Playa Estacahuite."

"Can you tell me how to get there?"

"Just follow the main road out of town and about thirty miles later you will be there."

"How will I find him once I get there?"

"Sorry, Senor. That is all I can tell you - the rest is up to you."

"Thank you."

As Jason was leaving the store, the clerk called after him, "Senor! Senor! Juan asked me to tell you that he is expecting you."

The Trade - Off

"A consistent man believes in destiny, a capricious man in chance."

Benjamin Disraeli

- Chapter Four -

Jason arrived at Playa Estacahuite later that morning - the clerk had not exaggerated the size of the town. He entered what appeared to be a broken-down saloon. The only person in the shack looked like one of the bandits referred to by the car rental attendant. Jason asked him where he might find a Juan Lopez. The man did not speak any English, so after several attempts, Jason finally determined that he did not know a Juan Lopez. Discouraged, Jason left the building and wondered what to do next. He wanted to be on his way home by evening - one day in this remote part of the world was enough for him.

As he walked up the street to another shack, he noticed a new Jeep Cherokee parked in front. He went in and was pleasantly surprised to find an American couple having lunch. They were from a small town north of Sante Fe, New Mexico. He asked if he could join them

The Trade - Off

for lunch. During the conversation that followed, he discovered that they were here to discuss attending next year's retreat with Juan. They said he could follow them to the site after they had finished their lunch.

Finally, Jason thought - progress.

They left the premises and headed east into the mountains that surrounded the small town. It was a beautiful day - clear blue sky, bright summer sun and a light breeze coming from the mountains west of the town. They arrived at a small clearing, which was surrounded by small lean-tos. In the center was a circular set of wooden benches that surrounded a stone firepit. In any other circumstances, Jason would have enjoyed the beautiful view of the valley below, but his mind was on other things.

There was a small group of people seated around the firepit in conversation. When Jason's group arrived, one of the participants in the discussion rose and came to greet them. He took one look at

Jason and said, "Welcome Jason. I am so happy you decided to come. We have much to discuss. Please join us here in the circle."

"Who are you?" Jason asked.

"I am Juan. I am the reason you are here. Frank sends his good wishes and has asked me to tell you that he hopes your visit here will be enlightening."

Jason's first reaction to meeting Juan was that there was something very familiar about him. He couldn't place exactly what, but he knew he had met him somewhere before.

"Is Frank here?"

"No, Senor. He left many weeks ago for South America. I do not expect him to return here for several months."

"Please Jason, join us. We have so much to cover and we need to begin or your stay here will be longer than you had planned."

"I plan to be here for one day only, Mr. Lopez."

"Please call me Juan, and you will be here much longer than that, my friend, if you want to make your journey worthwhile."

The Trade - Off

"Juan, I don't even know why I am here. Why would I need to stay longer than one afternoon?"

"You will see, my friend. Please sit."

There was a total of 12 people seated around the circle. They all introduced themselves. Except for himself and the couple with whom he came, the rest of the group was of different nationalities. There were five Orientals, three Canadians, and four Europeans. All spoke excellent English so, fortunately, Jason was able to understand the conversation. For the first hour, Jason only listened. The group was discussing the relationship between decisions, actions, choices and consequences. Each gave examples from their own life stories where poor decisions had yielded poor outcomes. Decisions that would have been different if they had known the eventual consequences.

Impatient now, Jason finally spoke up. "What is the point of this discussion?"

"Jason, have you any regrets in your life?" one of the Canadians asked.

"I have only just met each of you. I am not sure that I am willing to share my personal life story with you."

"That is your choice. However, if you choose not to participate, why are you here?"

"Good question. I don't know."

Juan spoke up, "He is here at my invitation."

"Why did you invite him?" someone asked.

"Because he is about to experience a terrible tragedy in his life which could be avoided. He will need to learn to see the relationship between his choices and his outcomes if he is to learn from this event and not repeat the same behavior."

Jason was surprised, curious, angry and incredulous all at the same time. "What do you mean, Juan, I am going to experience a terrible tragedy? Are you a psychic or fortuneteller of some kind? We have just met, you know nothing about me."

The Trade - Off

"Jason, please be patient and let me bring you up to date. We have all been here for several days discussing the recent discovery of a Mayan treasure that I found quite by accident several months ago. This discovery was of Ten Life Principles that this culture used thousands of years ago to create and build a society that, to this day, baffles men of science, the arts and literature. Somehow, the Mayan culture knew things that they shouldn't have been able to know at that time. They used techniques in agriculture, manufacturing, astronomy, and construction that were not invented until many centuries later. How did they possess knowledge, use it to create a successful working society, and then, for no apparent reason, disappear off the face of the Earth without a trace? Researchers have been studying many of their techniques. We are still learning new things every day with the additional daily excavation of their ruins. I discovered the Ten Life Principles late one day when I was leaving a spot where I often meditate.

"We have been discussing the Principles all week and are now on the final one. We are going to take a mid-afternoon break. Jason, please come with me to my hut. I want to share something with you that will change your future forever. I would like to give you a brief summary of nine of The Ten Principles."

The group left the circle and Jason followed Juan to his hut. When they entered, Juan asked him to be seated as he pulled out the tablet that contained The Ten Life Principles etched neatly in a language Jason did not recognize.

"I have translated the Principles into English and summarized them for our group. Their simplicity will amaze you."

The Trade - Off

"All the great things are simple."

Winston Churchill

Tim Connor

- *Ten Life Principles* -

1. *Always deal only in the truth.*
2. *Make wise and thoughtful choices.*
3. *Live a simple, yet purposeful life.*
4. *Let your wisdom give you understanding.*
5. *Honor nature and all of its creations.*
6. *Build a strong inner character.*
7. *Let humility replace your ego and arrogance.*
8. *Practice forgiveness in all of your relationships.*
9. *With gratitude you will inherit all things.*
10. *Always remember - love is all that matters.*

The Trade - Off

"Every day we ought to renew our purpose."

Thomas a Kempis

Chapter Five

"Jason, let me take a few moments to review the meaning of the Nine Principles and then we will spend some time tomorrow discussing Principle Number Two. If after this evening's discussion you feel that your trip was a waste of your time, I will send you home with my blessing. However, if you feel that more time here would be to your advantage, will you agree now to stay as long as necessary?"

"Juan, how can I make that kind of a commitment before I know what we are going to discuss?"

"Jason, you must learn faith, trust and patience. I ask you again will you stay?"

"Juan, I have business commitments at home that need my attention. I have a family that I miss and misses me. I have a life back in The United States."

The Trade - Off

"The rest of your life, if you choose to stay, will be more fulfilling, joyous and productive. That is all I can tell you. Your decision, Jason?"

Jason was in the midst of a déja vu. The last time he saw Frank, he asked him to make the decision of his life. What Frank never knew was that Jason was going to turn down Frank's offer to head the expansion project. But, what Jason recalled was Frank's remark, "I need the decision this morning. You have no time. Decide."

"I will stay as long as I feel the visit continues to be worthwhile."
"No, Jason. You will stay until your work is finished. Yes or no?"
"I will stay."

Jason's decision was not a rational one. In fact, as he contemplated that decision after many years, he never could understand why he chose to stay. He had just met Juan. But he had trusted Frank. There was something else, though. Juan had a peacefulness, a serenity about him. He exuded love, calmness and compassion.

"Very well, let us begin a brief overview of the nine Principles.

Principle Number One says: Always deal only in the truth.

This Principle is about your word, your integrity and your ethics. Without these as your foundation, you can never achieve greatness, happiness or any sense of peace. You will always wonder whom you should be, how you should behave, what you should share with others and what you should believe. Without this Principle as your guiding principle, you will lack the ability to effectively influence and persuade others, know your real self and project any type of moral or ethical code. No one will trust you. Oh, they will say they do, but do not be fooled. The ability to present falsities is never hidden deeply. We betray ourselves at every turn. Your work, your ideals, your relationships will lack any real deep meaning. You will miss the joy, passion and satisfaction without the daily practice of this Principle."

"Any questions Jason?"
"No."

The Trade - Off

"Are you still with me?"

"Yes, I was just thinking about how many times in life I have short-changed myself by not being more true to my word and the truth."

"Then let's move to the Third Principle, **Live a simple, yet purposeful life.**

This principle discusses how many people tend to complicate their lives with a variety of emotional, physical, personal and career issues and possessions. Life was meant to be joyous - not stressful; loving - not envious; caring - not selfish; abundant - not filled with scarcity; and simple - not packed every minute of every day with things to do, learn, see and buy. Simplicity is not about more; it is about less - not about better; but good - not about bigger; but acceptable - and not about beating others; but sharing with others.

As Man has progressed through the ages, he has searched for a better life for himself and his loved ones. In his search, somewhere along the way, he lost sight of what is really important in life - and it is not more of anything, but acceptance of what is.

Tim Connor

This is discussed more in a later principle, so I will move on to the final message in This Principle. It is the simple fact that history has proven time and time again that the people who have lived simple lives have contributed more to the lasting benefit of Man and his ability to find peace, harmony, balance and love.

Jason, clutter complicates life. Faster, more, better - complicates life. All of these create more opportunities for decisions, choices and actions. As a result of these additional opportunities, Man has a greater chance of making poor choices and suffering consequences at some future time. All of this is covered in The Second Principle, so, if you have no comments or questions, I will now summarize the Fourth Principle: **Let your wisdom give you understanding.**

The Fourth Principle discusses the difference between wisdom and knowledge, and knowledge and understanding. Knowledge is the awareness of information that one has gained through a variety of methods - formal education, experience, meditation and personal study. Wisdom is much deeper than knowledge. Wisdom is the awareness of why you know what you know and what value it has for you either now or in the future. Understanding is even deeper than wisdom. It is when you know something, you know why you know it and you know how you will use the

The Trade - Off

information in your life or experiences to improve your choices, decisions and actions. Many people have knowledge, much of which does them no good whatsoever. Others have gained wisdom from their knowledge, but lack understanding. Only those who have all three - knowledge, wisdom and understanding - have the power to make wise choices that will have a positive impact on the rest of their life.

Jason, why don't I stop for a moment and let you give me your reaction to or feelings about these first three Principles."

"I am overwhelmed. I never realized the significance of what contributes to all of the little daily outcomes and major life decisions. I have always thought carefully about my choices, but I now see I never fully understood the consequences of ignorance of the principles of making decisions and choices."

"Shall I go on?"

"Please continue with The Fifth Principle."

Juan continued, **Principle Number Five says, Honor Nature and All of its Creations.**

Tim Connor

The Earth, sky, seas and universe have been here for millions of years. Recently, the past one hundred years or less, Mankind has abused his home, his neighbors and the other creatures with whom he shares his home: from the smallest insect in the ground to the greatest mammal that roams in the forests and jungles. Man is the caretaker of his home and he has lost respect for nature, life as it is and life as it one day might become. In the process, he has lost respect for himself and his purpose. Life is eternal, the Soul is endless, and the spirit lives on in the trees, the grass and the soil. Man can kill his home if he chooses, but he can never destroy his spirit. He can end life as he has known it for centuries on Mother Earth, or he can learn to make better choices and decisions so that life will support coming generations for many more centuries. Man is at a crossroads. He must begin to make better choices soon or it will be too late for us all.

Jason, it is getting late. We need to conclude our evening discussions with the group so they can be on their way in the morning. Let us continue our review of the final five Principles later."

"Do you want me to join the group?"

The Trade - Off

"No, we will be concluding the retreat this evening with the final Principle. It would be wise for you to get some rest. You will need it.

"You may share my hut with me. There is an extra cot for your use. It is quite primitive here, but we have all that we need to survive and complete our purpose. Please make yourself comfortable. I will return later this evening after we have concluded our retreat, and we can finish our review of the last five Principles."

Juan was leaving the hut as his departing words reverberated through Jason's mind.

Jason thought, "Juan has referred twice to concluding the discussion with the final five Principles, but there are really six left. I wonder why he keeps leaving one out. He did say we would cover only nine of The Principles and leave the final one, number two, for a later time. I wonder what the significance of number two is?"

He decided to read Principle Number Two. When he finished, he sat down on the small cot and reflected on his early life and the many decisions he had made and how they all turned out. The thought kept creeping into the front of Jason's mind, "I never really thought my life would turn out this way."

And then he heard the echo of Cin's voice in the farthest corner of his mind, with words that would one day haunt him, "Jason, please, before it is too late for us."

The Trade - Off

"Rejoice in your hope, be patient in tribulation, be constant in prayer."

Romans 12:12

Chapter Six

When Juan woke Jason, the sun was already well above the horizon. He suggested that they have something to eat and continue their discussion of the principles outside.

Jason noticed that all of the other guests were gone and the camp was deserted. He and Juan were alone. Suddenly, everything sounded deathly quiet.

"Where have the other people gone?"

"The retreat has ended. They have returned to their lives, but each has taken a piece of this place with them. They will return to the routines of their life, but none of them will ever be the same. This retreat was the final stage in a life-long spiritual journey for each of them toward peace and understanding. You were sleeping so soundly last night that I decided not to disturb you. So now we must continue our work together.

Principle Number Six: Build a Strong inner Character.

This principle states that each of us is tested in our lives by many people, circumstances and experiences. Each of us has an inner code that we follow in all circumstances regarding behavior, beliefs and attitudes. This code was developed within us as a result of the exposure to our early environment, our teachers (and not just our formal teachers), our early life lessons, and finally, our learned reactions and responses to life's issues. Our character is like a thread that runs through us into everything and every person we touch from the day we first realize we have a choice as to what we believe and how we will behave. This thread is never broken. It can be stretched tight as we question our values and beliefs, and it can be strengthened as we develop maturity, inner knowledge, emotional health and spiritual courage. This last quality, spiritual courage, confuses many people. The others, although often difficult to maintain, are easy to understand. Spiritual courage is the ability to maintain congruence between who you believe you are and who you are becoming. Each of us is confronted with the opportunity to learn about the world, ourselves, and life itself. As we gain in wisdom and understanding, we leave old beliefs behind and embrace new

Tim Connor

ones. This transition for many is difficult. They see it as the transition of their character, from the old to the new. But this is not so. The old is intricately woven into the new. What you once were is still a part of who you are. What you once believed has shaped what you now believe. Finally, character is who you are when you are alone. It is not how you behave when you think you should act in certain ways, or even how you behave when others are watching; but it is who you are when no one but you knows or will ever know - your actions, decisions, and choices.

Your reaction please, Jason."

"Juan, I have spent my entire adult life in search of success, freedom and independence. During this time there have always been situations causing me to go against my inner guidance system and take an action or make a decision that at the time seem justified - but later, when I re-evaluated it, I realized that I had compromised a little of myself. I have known all along what character is and how important it is to inner peace and harmony. But I must say that I have not always been able to practice what I believed. Your reminder today, with this Sixth Principle, is like a gentle, yet necessary mental lightning bolt that has reached deep into my inner being. It has placed in front of me my lack of integrity, and congruence, that what I stand for has any meaning for me personally. It is almost as if I were teaching this to others, but not with my deeds, only my words. I am beginning to get a glimpse of why Frank suggested to you that I spend time with you."

Let's move on to The Seventh Principle.

Principle Number Seven says that Humility is not Weakness, but Strength.

It goes on to explain that if a person is humble it should not be taken as a sign of inferiority, lack of power, lack of knowledge or understanding. Many people wrongly believe that humility is a sign of emotional and physical weakness, that this person is a servant of others, a person who lacks any ability to influence others during the course of their life. This assumption is very wrong. The ability to be humble carries with it a great burden and responsibility. The burden is to accept other people's incorrect assessments and often their verbal abuse with a quiet sense of dignity, compassion, understanding and forgiveness. The responsibility is to understand that it is not the powerful, the famous or the wealthy that will determine Man's ultimate outcome as he moves slowly yet relentlessly into his future - but the servants, teachers, poets, spiritual leaders, workers, and children. You see, the servant is really the master and the master the servant. All of the ancient spiritual teachers have suggested that it is the meek, the humble, the downtrodden, and the needy who will inherit the riches of the Kingdom - not the business leader, the politician or the wealthy. Many people today have misunderstood this Principle and have followed the desires of their ego and mind rather than their heart and soul. Humility is the ability to touch others in a positive way without concern for reward, appreciation or even acknowledgment.

Jason, we don't have much time left and I want to complete this brief overview of the Nine Principles so we can finally get to principle Number Two and the reason for your trip. Although this discussion might ultimately prove valuable for you, we need to complete our work so that you can return home soon.

Principle Number Eight says: Practice Forgiveness in all of your Relationships.

It is very difficult for many people to practice this principle. In the real world, there are people who hurt others by their words, deeds, selfishness, ignorance and arrogance. Everyone is good at his soul level. It is at the conscious level of actions where many people go astray and let their ego, pride, fear, pain, grief and needs control their beliefs and behavior. As a

The Trade - Off

result, some people either consciously or unconsciously hurt others in a variety of ways. It takes courage, humility, love, maturity and a peaceful center to forgive another when they have wronged you in some way either deliberately or accidentally. Either way the outcome is the same – the person inflicted some emotional or physical pain. To let go of this is not an easy task. Some people can be heard saying, 'I will or I can never forgive that person for their action or actions.' or, 'I will carry this burden to my grave.' or any similar phrase. What these people fail to realize is that their lack of forgiveness for the other person, a person whom they do not generally like or respect, now has taken over the other parts of their life, career or relationships. This lack of forgiveness now gives power to this person over the remainder of the other person's life, sometimes called the 'victim.' These people are victims because they have chosen to see themselves so. They are really victims of their own thoughts, beliefs and feelings. No one can take control of our thoughts unless we choose to give it to them. They can torture, punish, threaten, abandon, or any other negative action and we can, if we choose and remain true to ourselves, withstand these onslaughts. It is unfortunate that many people have not yet discovered that they have this power. As a result, many of these people can easily fall prey to these so-called 'evil' people, deeds or actions. For many years, there has been a belief *in love as positive and powerful and evil as negative and powerful. Neither of these exists in the world. They exist in Man himself. Man can choose to behave in a loving or evil way, but you must remember that all of life is a perceptual interpretation; that one person's definition of love may differ from another, and one person's definition of evil or wrong-doing may differ from another. There must, therefore, be a higher rule or principle and it is this principle that permits man to rise above his own negative deeds and those of his fellow man. He can only do this with forgiveness - total, complete and lasting forgiveness. The ability to forgive is found within the divine nature of all of us. Therefore, if a person says they cannot forgive they are denying their own inner divine nature. And that is not God's purpose here on this earth plane."*

"Juan, I have many questions about these principles that I would like to discuss with you. I am beginning to feel overwhelmed by all of this new insight."

"Please Jason, we will have ample time for your questions. Let's complete the nine principles and then we can discuss any that you have questions or concerns about in greater detail.

The Trade - Off

Principle Number Nine says: With Gratitude you will inherit all things.

We all have much for which to be grateful. The list is too endless to give to you in this principle. Just keep in mind that, although there are times when you feel discouraged, filled with grief, and unable to see beyond your current negative circumstances, there is always something in your life for which to be thankful. It is at these low points in your life that your ability to be grateful is challenged. Courage is the ability to carry on no matter what negative appearances may fill your days or your thoughts. People who have lost the ability to be grateful have lost hope, patience, faith and an understanding about the real nature of life. Life is not joyous, happy, good, bad, or any other condition. Life is a neutral experience that each of us fills with whatever is dominant in our minds at any given time. If you feel lack, you will create space for more lack. If you feel joy you will open the channels for life to give you more joy. If you feel positive inside, regardless of what is happening outside, you become like a magnet that will shower you with what you resonate out to the world from your inner being. But, this law can also work against you. If you let these outer conditions control your inner beliefs and attitudes, you will shut down the flow of abundance into your life. The Principle does not play favorites. It doesn't shower some people with more and others with less because they want them, feel they deserve them, or ask for them. One must create and maintain an inner feeling of gratitude that is consistent no matter what is being felt or experienced.

And Finally, Principle Number Ten says: Love is All That Matters. It has been said that there are only two emotions – love and hate. Both of these reside within the individual. You cannot love some things and hate others. You cannot hate some things and love others. You are either filled with love and its cousins: joy, compassion, happiness, faith, patience, wonder, and passion - or you are filled with hate and its offspring: grief, fear, jealousy, worry, blame, pain, greed and resentment. You must choose your dominant inner environment. You cannot vacillate. You cannot have it both ways. You cannot choose to be one way at certain times in your life or with certain people - then another at other times. You must be consistent if you want this principle to work in your life. You cannot have a vacuum in your consciousness. If you choose love, there is no room for hate. If you choose hate, you leave no room for love to enter. It is unfortunate that many people have made this choice without any understanding of why or how it influences all of their decisions, actions and choices.

The Trade - Off

Let's stop for a while, Jason, there is something interesting you must see before we continue."

Tim Connor

> *"Take care to get what you like or you will be forced to like what you get."*

George Bernard Shaw

The Trade - Off

Chapter Seven

Juan led Jason into the woods just behind the camp. There was a small narrow path that looked like it had been used fairly frequently. The overhanging trees made it appear as if they were heading into a long tunnel. It was still mid-day but in the forest it could have easily been dusk. Shadows from the trees and branches moved constantly giving an eerie feeling to the woods. It was as if they were alive. They walked for an hour or two without exchanging a word. Juan seemed to know where he was going as he walked on confidently without hesitation. They stopped to rest for a few minutes, but then continued their walk deeper into the forest. The sun peeked in and out of the trees overhead and Jason could see that the sun was now at around 3PM. His concern was that if they continued they would be returning in total darkness.

"Juan, how much farther are we going?"

"It is just around the next bend."

It seemed to take an another hour to reach the point that Juan had mentioned. When they reached it, the trees opened up and gave way to a large area about the size of seven or eight football fields. There were a number of ancient ruins as well as several working excavation sites within the confines of what must have been, at one time, a city.

"What is this?"

"This is an ancient Mayan city that was recently discovered. The excavations have not yet yielded any recognizable signs as to the date of origin, who lived here, when they left or even a name of the city. The history books make no mention of these ruins or any major Mayan city this far south in Mexico. There are a few ancient ruins in Central America, but no one is sure of the significance of this particular discovery."

"Why have we come?"

The Trade - Off

"There is something you must see while you are here. It may shed some light on the reason for your visit. Please come with me."

They headed for the center of the city. There was an old structure that had been the benefactor of hundreds, maybe thousands, of years of wear and tear from the wind, rain and pollution There was a clearly identified opening in the middle that must have at one time been the entrance. Once inside the building, it looked like an ancient place of worship. There was what appeared to be some kind of altar at the center of the large open area. A seating area, a series of concentric circular risers, surrounded the altar. They were crumbling and were no longer usable for seating. As they approached the altar, something strange began to happen to Jason, something that many years later Jason was still unable to explain. He had a vision. He had never had one in his life. He didn't even believe in them. He didn't even know it was a vision, but he didn't know what else to call it. Cin had spent many hours through the years with a variety of psychics, dream therapists, channels and Yoga instructors. She was much more comfortable with 'the other side.' Jason, like most people, was extremely skeptical of what he did not understand.

Yes, he had been a very active dreamer with his unconscious trying to warn him of impending future events. But he had never found a suitable or acceptable answer to any of his dreams. He had become so concerned that he had put his prejudice behind and had spent some time with a dream therapist, but it proved of no value and he discontinued his sessions.

While in the building, Jason seemed to be totally suspended in real time. It was as if he were no longer living his life, but became a part of the vision itself. A very strange experience, it seemed to last for several minutes. When it ended and Jason returned to the present moment, Juan was nowhere in sight. Jason called to him, but there was no answer. He called again louder, with a hint of panic in his voice – still nothing. He left the building and realized that he must have been there longer than he had originally thought. His present

The Trade - Off

circumstances overshadowed any urgent need to understand the vision and its meaning better.

The sun was almost completely below his line of sight now and a few early evening shadows visible from where he stood with a thin line of red light just barley visible above the horizon. He had no flashlight, matches, food or water. He didn't know where he was, and for the first time in his life, he felt real fear, gut-wrenching fear. As he considered his next move, he realized that he might have to spend the night in this ancient city where only ghosts of a time long past would be his companions.

For several minutes he wandered aimlessly around the city, stumbling over rocks and broken tree limbs, and quickly came to the conclusion that this was a useless waste of time. He didn't know what he expected to find or where he was going, so, rather than injure himself, he found a large old tree that seemed to reach the stars and settled in under its large branches for protection.

Tim Connor

The clear night sky was filled with millions of white dots from one horizon to the next. The full moon enabled him to see some distance - if not the details of what he was seeing, at least something or someone approaching. He sat there and contemplated his career, relationships and life in general and slowly fell off into a deep sleep.

Characters floated in and out of his dream-state with no rhyme or reason, but there was some relationship among them. Frank was the first one to appear; then Cinamon. His mother and Marjorie seemed to play major roles. Juan wandered in very early as well, along with Frank's wife, Mary. The children also made cameo appearances with several friends and customers. Each had served a specific purpose in his life. They were all there to help him learn what seemed to be one lesson, 'make wise and careful decisions' – both the major and seemingly insignificant ones will determine your life. Juan, however, seemed to play the major role. He was there with him from his first major choice through his most recent one. He would give Jason a warm satisfying smile from somewhere deep in his consciousness when he made a right choice and would just as

The Trade - Off

lovingly send him a scowl when he made a poor choice. Juan was Jason's Spirit Guide, although Jason never really knew of his presence in his conscious mind while he was living his life. Jason always seemed to sense a gentle unconscious nudge no matter what decision he made or action he took. It didn't seem to matter what choices he made, everything turned out as it was supposed to, in spite of Jason's ignorance, arrogance, or refusal to learn. It didn't always turn out the way he would have wished or expected, but he came to realize that the outcomes were consistent with his choices. He hadn't learned yet about the idea of the spiritual side of life; that there are many things that cannot be explained with logic, scientific method and evidence.

The dream suddenly took a dramatic turn. Everything went haywire. The characters seemed to turn on Jason for no apparent reason. They were no longer loving, kind or pleasant. Even his children became hostile. What began as a pleasant dream experience quickly became a horrible nightmare.

Tim Connor

"Courage is the capacity to confront what can be imagined."

Leo Rosten

The Trade - Off

- Chapter Eight -

Jason's life began to slowly unravel - first it was his marriage, then his other relationships, then his career, and, finally, his health - all fell apart. One by one, he was permitted to see how each individual decision he made either consciously or unconsciously had an impact on some aspect of his future. The final episode took place while Jason and his family were sailing in the Caribbean on vacation. Jason was an average sailor. He could handle the boat reasonably well and his navigation skills were enough to get them there and back. But something happened that haunts Jason's every moment. A brief squall came out of nowhere while they were a few miles offshore of one of the Virgin Island's smaller islands. The winds increased, the rain was incessant and the sea was like an angry animal. When the mast broke and came thundering down on Cin and the children, Jason couldn't believe his eyes. He screamed for them to get out of the way, but the wind swallowed his warning. The last thing he thought, as he watched in horror as his family was about to be smashed to bits, was that Cin wanted to go to the mountains this year on vacation and not sailing.

He was getting a rare glimpse of how one's decisions directly and indirectly influence some area of one's future.

Juan was there every step of the way trying to guide him. There were times when he even used coercion to attempt to help Jason see in advance how his choice would change the rest of his life.

"Jason," Juan counseled, "do you remember when you were in high school and were in excellent physical condition?"
"Yes."
"Do you remember when you chose to stop exercising?"
"No, I don't recall that I actually made a conscious choice."
"You are right, but don't you remember how you let the little things day by day get in the way of your earlier physical routines? You used to run two to three days a week. You worked out at the gym once or twice a week. Then gradually you eliminated these

The Trade - Off

behaviors - convincing yourself that other things like dating Cinnamon, attending social functions, and studying left you no time for exercise. Years later, with your career and with your children, you lacked the energy to give to these activities and people. You would come home from a long hard day, exhausted and unable to devote any of yourself to Jeff and Cindy. You would often lose mental concentration at work, thereby cheating yourself of your best efforts. All because you let your body, that perfect physical being you were given, lose its capacity for endurance. You chose to put some things in front of others and you paid the price later."

"But Juan, there wasn't time for everything. Something had to give. I couldn't be all things to everyone - including myself."

"Jason, don't you realize that if you don't take care of your body, your body will not be able to take care of you when you most need it?"

"Juan, you just don't understand the trade-offs I had to make."

"Jason, I understand that you made these trade-offs, as you call them, unknowingly. You traded off a piece of your future for something that you believed was more important in your present. Let me give you another example.

"Do you remember when you were deciding on a college to attend?"

"Yes, I recall that one college would be closer to home, but would not give me the opportunities for study that the other ones I was considering had. I chose to attend the college that was several hundred miles from home."

"And do you remember the price you paid for that decision?"

"Wait a minute Juan. Are you telling me that I made a wrong decision?"

"Jason, there are no wrong decisions in life. The thing we must remember is that each decision gets us an entirely different set of outcomes. One decision – one set of consequences; another decision - a completely different set."

"Then I don't know what you are getting at. I chose that college because it was where I wanted to go. How could I see the future to know what consequences I would get as a result of it?"

The Trade - Off

"You are quite right Jason. No one can ever know the outcomes of the decisions they make. Some people drink alcohol for years and live to a ripe old age. Others who drink end up with a variety of health problems and sometimes an early death. Who is to know? Who is to say what is better? But, there are signs along the way. There is such a thing as common sense and good judgment. There is better awareness. There is paying attention. There is knowledge. And finally, there is always a price either sooner or later. The person, for example, who drinks a great deal. Might they not pay a price in their social relationships, their career or their personal relationships? Let's get back to our college example. What price did you pay to go away to college?"

"I missed my brother's high school graduation. I wasn't able to be there for my mother when my father was ill."

"Your father passed away at a relatively young age, did he not?"

"Yes."

"How old was he when he died?"

"Forty-eight."

"What caused his death?"

"My father never exercised, had a poor diet and smoked most of his life. He was warned by many doctors that if he did not change his lifestyle he would most likely not have a full life."

"Your father also then made many choices and decisions thinking he could outwit the consequences?"

"Yes, I suppose he did."

"And your mother? How did she handle the next several years?"

"She never was able to overcome the grief of losing my father. She spent the next several years fighting the health effects of depression."

"What ultimately happened to her?"

"She is now an old, bitter woman unable to receive or share love with her family and friends. It is very sad and I have tried over the years to help her, but she has chosen to remain stuck in this destructive pattern."

"Then she, too, has made many choices and is now experiencing the outcomes."

"Yes, she is alone, lonely, broken-hearted, and aging very rapidly."

The Trade - Off

"Is there more?"

"Yes, I wasn't able to introduce Cinnamon to my father before he died."

"How do you feel about that?"

"I have carried a burden since then."

"Why? As you have said you couldn't have known that your father would become ill and pass away while you were at school. You couldn't know you would meet Cinamon at college. You couldn't know that the family finances would not be able to support you your last two years at school, leaving you to scrape and scrounge to survive. Whereas, if you had been closer to home, things would have been different. When your father died suddenly, you could not be at his bedside. You could not console your mother during that difficult time. You could not be there for your brother when he needed a male role model more than ever."

"Was I supposed to sacrifice my life - not knowing these future possibilities?"

"That is not my point Jason. You carry guilt, pain, anger and resentment toward yourself because of your decision. That is all. These inner feelings have indirectly sabotaged your success in many areas of your life."

"I have been quite successful, Juan."

"Financially, yes. But at what price?"

"What do you mean?"

"Your relationship with your wife is not all that great now, is it?"

"It is as good as can be expected - given the circumstances I faced."

"Now we are getting somewhere. The circumstances, as you call them, were of your own making. You created them as a result of your early choices - all of them. Can't you see that Jason?"

"No, I can't. I did the best I could at the time with what I knew at the time."

"Did you?"

"Yes I believe I did."

"Why?"

The Trade - Off

"Juan, how could I have known of these other potential circumstances as a result of making different decisions earlier?"

"Well, my friend, I believe we are finally making some progress. Now tell me about your relationship with Marjorie while in high school."

"We were good friends, that's all."

"Did you ever see her after graduation?"

"No."

"Why not?"

"We lost track of each other, that's all. Why?"

"Did you know that Marjorie never graduated from Harvard?"

"Why didn't she?"

"She failed out. Couldn't take the stress and pressure."

"What happened to her?"

"Do you really want to know?"

"Yes."

"After leaving school, she secured a position with an international organization like the Peace Corps in the sixties. She was in a remote part of the world trying to 'find herself' while helping others. She was in a small plane flying to a very remote site in Brazil when her plane crashed and she was killed. There was a funeral in your home town, but you were not there, were you?"

"Oh God, no"

"Yes, Jason, your best friend is dead. And you didn't even attend the funeral did you?"

"You know I didn't."

"Why didn't you keep in touch with her?"

" I don't know, just never got around to it."

"You just never took the time. You chose not to. Not a conscious choice to not call or write, but a choice of inaction just the same – which, my friend, ultimately has the same consequences."

At that point in Jason's dream, Cinamon became the lead character. She was attending one of Cindy's school functions. Jason could not be there. He was working late. He had told Cin he would try and make it, but she had learned that Jason's promises were worthless. He just attempted in vain to pacify her. When Jason got home from

The Trade - Off

work late that day, she was packed and ready to leave. She had had enough.

Jason was suddenly brought back to consciousness by a loud crack of lightning that struck the tree he had used for shelter.

As he looked up, he saw to his horror that one of the main branches had split off from the tree and was falling quickly on a direct path toward him. He attempted to scurry to safety, but he was too late.

Tim Connor

"Smooth seas do not make skillful sailors."

African Proverb

Chapter Nine

Jason sat up unhurt and looked at the tree above him. The branch had broken lose and fallen toward him. It lay on the ground next to him a few feet away. But he was not touched. How had he escaped certain injury? How did the branch miss him and land next to him and not on him? He was mystified. As he was looking at the fallen branch he felt a presence behind him. He turned and it was Juan. He had just appeared as if out of thin air.

"Juan, where did you come from?"

"I have been here all along. You just chose not to see me."

"How, Juan, could I choose not to see you?"

"I can give you a common and really somewhat humorous example. Has your wife ever asked you to go to the kitchen or basement to get something and you stood looking carefully at all of the contents of the cabinet and proudly declared it wasn't there or you couldn't find it?"

"Many times."

"Then your wife or even one of your children comes to your aid - opens the cabinet and selects the item within a few seconds. How did you feel at those times?"

"A little stupid or embarrassed."

"Was the item there all the time?"

"Yes."

"Why were you unable to see it after several seconds of looking?"

"I don't know."

"It is called selective vision in some circles or professions and non-selective vision in others. We have chosen to call it temporary isolation. You have temporarily, for some reason, chosen to isolate the event or circumstance from your active consciousness. Your unconscious seeing eye sees the item immediately, but is temporarily overruled by your conscious mind – therefore you really see it but you don't see it. Is that clear?"

"What is the point Juan? And who are the "we" to whom you referred?"

The Trade - Off

"One at a time, my friend. There are many times in a person's life when he has temporary isolation - when he is dating and looking for a life partner or lover and he sees certain traits but misses others. Children are perfect in the eyes of their parents or grandparents, but not in the sight of neighbors or teachers. Have you ever interviewed a potential employee and seen only what you wanted to see?"

"Many times. But, why do we do this, this temporary isolation?"

"For some it is a protective mental device to shield them from negative memories. For others, they have just chosen to not pay attention or, to put it another way, they have chosen to pay more conscious attention to one thing than another at that time. For example, when you were looking in the cabinet, your mind was focused more actively on something else than on seeing what your wife wanted you to get. Your unconscious mind can take it all in simultaneously. It sees what your conscious does not see. It hears what your ears do not hear. It remembers what you do not remember experiencing. On the other hand, your conscious mind must focus on one thing at a time. If you try to focus on three tasks, you will not be as effective as you could have been because in one of those tasks you will be present in the present moment, but in the others you will be in the past or future moments. And you cannot be effective in the past or future, only the now moments of your life."

"Juan, are you telling me that I can't walk, chew gum and have a conversation at the same time?"

"No, I am not saying that. I am saying that if you do all of these - two of the three will get short-changed. Have you ever missed an exit off the highway for your home, when you have been taking it for several years?"

"I see what you mean now. But what does all of this have to do with you appearing behind me - or the tree limb?"

"If you will let me, I will be happy to explain."

"I am sorry. I had a strange nightmare while resting under the tree and I am a little shaken."

"That is why I am trying to help you understand. Your mind never sleeps. Some portion is always active. Your heart doesn't stop beating or you don't stop breathing while you are sleeping. Your unconscious mind continues to monitor and control every beat and every breath while you dream of sun-drenched beaches and cool

The Trade - Off

summer breezes. Your unconscious mind also is responsible for any dream states you experience. The question has been for many years - is the dreamer having a dream that he or she is participating in, or is the dream the reality and the dream is really what you believe is your daily active conscious life? In other words, is what you are experiencing now with me, this conversation, a dream - or was your conversation with me in what you thought was a dream actually reality?"

"Juan, that seems a little far out for me."

"Well it would explain one aspect of temporary isolation - why we don't see things consciously when they are there until they are pointed out to us. Once your daughter shows you the item in the cabinet, you now see it consciously.

"I was walking toward you for the past several minutes. You were not paying attention to anything other than the tree limb. This is not good or bad. It is just what you were doing at the time I was approaching. Therefore, you did not see or hear me until your focus was no longer on the tree, but open and receptive to your now moment and your environment. This, Jason, is one of the critical aspects of making wise choices and decisions; to remain open and receptive to what is - to reality - and to stay in the present moment and away from memories, the past, fantasy, and the future. One cannot make wise choices when only making them from experience.

A person also cannot make wise decisions when they are focused only on what could be, might be or will be in the future. It is important to use information from the past and the future while making decisions in the present, but it is even more vital to stay in touch with what you believe now, feel now and are experiencing now – to prevent selective isolation affecting your decisions, choices and actions. People who are not able to get out of selective isolation in their decision making tend to make poor or unwise decisions that negatively impact them in the future. Back to the limb. First. The tree limb did fall. We know that. Second. You were directly under the tree and it did not touch you. Third. The law of gravity is still in effect here in Mexico. So, why didn't the limb hit you? It's your turn, Jason."

"Using the logic of your explanation, Juan, I don't know."

The Trade - Off

"Then think out of the box Jason. You have been good at that in the past; don't abandon that thinking now."

"There must be some spiritual force in the universe that watches over us, some unseen guidance system that protects us from circumstances of which we are not aware."

"Can you give me a practical example?"

"Sure. I can remember driving home from work late one night, preoccupied with some serious business decision. I was not paying attention to my driving and remember thinking that I had traveled a good mile and a half without any conscious memory of driving through that part of town. What was strange later was I realized that there are several traffic lights that I went through without noticing. They could have been red or green. It doesn't matter. If they were red, I must have stopped and then moved on when they changed, but I didn't remember them, and yes, I know they are there. Some force must have been guiding my driving because I was not consciously aware of the time."

"How do you know?"

"Because my cellular phone rang and brought me out of the dreamlike state I was in and I noticed I was approaching a red light, my foot on the brakes, but I don't remember moving my foot from the accelerator to the brakes."

"You are correct with your evaluation. There are unseen forces in the universe that watch over us and can, if we are not careful, derail us. This is one of the advantages of staying in the present moment, fully conscious at all times. There is nothing wrong with daydreaming at times, but one must guard against going through life in this semi-conscious manner. Decisions often made at these times prove to be irrational or incorrect.

"So why didn't the limb strike you? Are you saying that your unconscious state was somehow passed to the limb and it knew that you would not move so it changed its course?"

"I don't know."

"Let me put it another way. If you make a decision while unconscious that impacts others, does your decision in some way alter their consciousness so that they either get in tune with or ally themselves against your decision and its outcomes?"

The Trade - Off

"I don't know what you mean."

"Let's say you make a decision to move from one area of the country to another. After you have made it, your wife either supports it or argues against it. What will be the determining factor in her attitude?"

"I am sure her opinion of my decision will also have some impact on the decision's consequences."

"Jason, we don't make decisions in a vacuum. Our decisions put into play an entire set of circumstances that we cannot control originating in the consciousness of other people. Your wife also makes decisions or choices and gets consequences as well. If you are not careful, you can let this concept become very complicated. In other words, you make a decision to move. She decides she does not want to, and you have disagreement. This ends in a set of circumstances in which she decides to leave you because she does not want to leave her friends, career and life, as she knows it. So you divorce. This decision on both of your parts now impacts the children, in-laws, friends, your career, lifestyle and future. What if you had decided not to move? Then you would not have the benefit or negative consequences of divorce as a result of your disagreement, but you would now put an entire new set of consequences into play. Do you see how this works?"

"Yes I believe I do. But I agree a person could go insane wondering about all of the ripple effects of any decision they made - no matter how large or small."

"You are right. That's why we want to keep this entire concept as simple as possible. Back to our example of the limb. If the limb had hit you - let's assume - and I don't like making assumptions, but for the sake of illustration let's assume that the limb would have killed you. What can we derive about your decision to come to Mexico to see me as a result of my invitation?"

"That I came to be here so that at the precise moment the limb fell I would be under it. Are you talking about fate here, Juan?"

"Call destiny what you want. I do not like to get hung up on the use of certain words to describe certain events or people. I would prefer to look deeper into the concept. Fate implies that no matter what choices a person makes, they have no control over the outcomes. In other words, if it were your time to die - under a tree in

The Trade - Off

Mexico - you would have been here whether I invited you or not. Some other set of circumstances would have led you to this ancient city and this tree at this particular time. You see, the limb fell when it did because of nature. You just happened to be here at the right or wrong time. You didn't cause the lightning; you didn't cause the particular limb to be vulnerable. You didn't control the weather patterns that led to the lightning and so on and so on."

"Juan, so how do fate and destiny differ when it comes to our conscious choices?"

"Are you familiar with the idea of - free will?"

"Of course."

"Then you answer the question, Jason."

Tim Connor

"*Even if you are on the right track, you'll get run over if you just sit there.*"

Will Rogers

Chapter Ten

Jason began, "Free will is the gift that God gives to every human. It is the ability to determine your destiny. Each of us is permitted the opportunity, as well as the right, to make any choice and take any action that we want at any time. We have the right to make poor choices that lead to negative consequences and we have the right to make wise choices that lead to positive outcomes. He doesn't interfere or intercede with the decisions each of us makes."

"So then God permits us to fail?"

"Yes."

"He also permits us to pay the price of those poor decisions?"

"Yes."

"Are we getting into a religious discussion here Juan?"

"Not exactly. God is not about any particular religion or religious doctrine but His primary concern for Man is his spiritual courage and ability to give and receive love. He permits each of us to grow and learn as we move through the days of our lives - one decision at a time. Anything else would be slavery, and it would take the control of a person's destiny out of his hands.

"So, Juan what does all of this have to do with limbs falling and lightning storms?"

"There is a force in the universe, as I have already told you, that somehow controls many aspects of nature and life. It is divine in nature. God created this perfect and harmonious universe - although some may doubt that fact - so that He could fulfill his divine nature in and through all things. No one, no matter how long or hard they investigate or study, will ever come close to understanding the true nature of life, consciousness, or God and the miracle of creation and life. Your time here is not yet complete. There is something you are to do or some purpose for you to fulfill. Otherwise, that limb would have sent you on your spiritual journey to another spirit plane. But there is more to this that you are not quite ready for yet. We will save it for another time. I would like to walk around the city for a while. Being here makes me feel, for some reason, that I am close to God. Come let's walk. We can discuss the final Principle, Number

The Trade - Off

Two, while we walk. It is a lovely day and we certainly won't be disturbed here."

They headed toward the far side of the city, taking a perimeter path that rimmed the outskirts of the center core of buildings. Every now and then they came across an old artifact that was evidence of an ancient culture long gone. Jason suddenly realized that he was hungry. They hadn't eaten anything since last evening's supper and it was now mid day.

"Juan, what are the chances of getting some water and something to eat? I am getting quite hungry."

"Learn to feed your heart and soul before you worry about feeding your body. You can miss a meal, even a few days of meals, but if you are spiritually hungry all of the food in the world won't give you peace or harmony in your life."

"Could we at least see if we can find some water?"

"Follow me, there is a well up ahead. We can stop and talk there."

Tim Connor

They found the well, dropped the bucket down slowly into the water, filled it, then retrieved it and each took several swallows of the cool fresh water. Jason noticed, however, that the water had a strange odor. It wasn't an unpleasant smell, almost sweet like the smell of fresh flowers. They found a grassy spot near the well and sat down comfortably facing each other.

"This well is used by the team that is conducting the excavation. They drilled it so they could have ample water. It gets quite hot here in the summer.

"Let's complete our discussion of the Ten Life Principles. **Principle Number Two says: make wise and thoughtful choices.**"

Jason began to feel dizzy and his vision began to blur. He said to Juan, "I feel strange. Is there something in that water? Do you feel anything Juan?"

"No, I am used to it, it will pass. Do not worry."

The Trade - Off

But the feelings did not pass, and Jason felt like he was sliding down a steep hill - losing control of his faculties and physical movements.

"It is getting worse, Juan, not better. I can hardly see you and you seem to have a glow around you. I feel lightheaded. What is causing this?"

"I told you, Jason, do not worry. It is a normal reaction to the water in this well. Everyone who drinks from it has the same experience."

Juan watched as Jason gradually lost consciousness. When he had completely left the present moment behind, Juan stood and gently placed his hands on Jason's head and began to speak in Spanish. When he was finished with his ritual, Jason suddenly regained consciousness and looked strangely at Juan.

Jason didn't speak for several minutes. And then he began, "I came here with skepticism in my heart. I believed that this journey was a waste of my time and came only out of obligation to Frank. I felt like some strange and unexplainable force was pulling me here. After I arrived, I was convinced that there was nothing to be gained by staying, but I decided I was willing to stay for one day since I had made the long trip. When you began your discussion of the Ten Principles, I felt an uneasy sense of déjà vu, as if I had been here before, and had lived through this experience at another time in my life. I don't know why or when, but at some point in the past twenty-four hours, I have come to believe that my future and all of its uncertainty is somehow clearer. I have been willing to drop my defenses, fears and doubts to open myself up to whatever possibilities are coming to me. I feel a tremendous sense of relief and inner peace that no matter what choices I make from now on - they will be the right ones. I don't know why or where this sense of completion is coming from, but I no longer feel at odds with life."

"Jason, let's complete our discussion of Principle Number Two and then you will understand. ***Principle Number Two says: Make Wise and Thoughtful Choices.***

The Trade - Off

"None of us can know the future. And, this is in our best interests. To know the future would dramatically impact our present. There would be some positive benefits from knowing the future. One could avoid poor judgment, mistakes and failure, but one would also lose the ability to learn from mistakes. There are three keys in this Principle.

- Key number one: Release the expected and embrace the unexpected.
- Key number two: Forget your mistakes, but remember their lessons.
- Key number three: The job of humans is not to make right decisions, but to learn to make right the decisions they make.

Key number one…

…release the expected and embrace the unexpected. It counsels us to accept life as it is given to us. Not with resignation that we can have no control over its outcomes, but with the acceptance of our consequences due to our decisions and actions. It advises us to carefully evaluate options but not to become attached to outcomes. Life can change in a heartbeat. It also reminds us that we are not *operating in a vacuum; that other people's decisions and actions indirectly interact with ours making it impossible to know the exact consequence of one our choices in advance. We are not victims unless we choose to see ourselves as such. When we become attached to outcomes, we set ourselves up for frustration, anxiety, stress and disappointment. Life is not perfect; it just is.*

Key number two...
...forget your mistakes - but remember their lessons.
Everyone makes mistakes. A person cannot escape the consequences of choices as the result of ignorance, arrogance or both. Everyone, at one time, uses poor judgment. He mistakenly chooses an option - thinking that he has no better options or no options at all. Everyone fails. No one is perfect. No one is right all of the time. No one has a special relationship with the Truth at all times. As a result, each of us - even the best of us - makes a mistake in evaluation, expectation or judgment sooner or later. The wise person knows that if he keeps the memory of his mistakes in his active conscious mind he will attract similar circumstances. We tend to bring into our life that to which we pay attention or focus on. These people have chosen to

The Trade - Off

accept the fact that they will make mistakes, but that to live a worthwhile life they must learn something from them. These people focus on the learning or the lesson rather than the mistake itself.

Key number three...
...our job, when it comes to decisions, is not to try and make right decisions or choices, but to make them and then make them right ones. This key urges us not to spend too much time worrying about decisions - so much that we waste time and thought energy in attempting to manipulate the outcome. One of the biggest mistakes people make in life is trying to make right decisions. The right career, the right business, the right relationship and so on... Who is to say - given all of the variables and time involved for a decision to come to fruition - what is the right choice? It also tells us that we can make what we believe are right decisions that can turn out wrong for some reason within or beyond our control, and we can make wrong decisions that turn out right. This key is designed to help us realize that we can get no consequences - either right or wrong - until we choose or decide and then act on our decision.

Tim Connor

"This key is the cause of all happiness, success, accomplishment, failure, frustration, broken dreams, relationship issues, financial problems and every other life circumstance. To understand it fully, we must look at a recent example in your life."

"OK, Juan. You have spent several hours sharing the Ten Principles with me and I appreciate your effort, guidance and patience. You have thoroughly convinced me of the importance of making good choices and decisions - regardless of whether they fall in the area of seemingly insignificant daily issues or the major life outcomes. However, you have not helped me one bit when it comes to learning how to make better choices. What good is the knowledge of the importance of wise choices if I don't know how to improve them?"

"You are quite right, my friend, and I plan to share with you the corresponding Ten Life Actions that are found on the back of the stone tablet that gave us the Principles. Whoever wrote those Principles was well aware of human nature. Knowledge of 'what is' is fine, but knowledge of 'how to' is just as valuable. I want to answer one of your earlier questions of who is the 'we' I spoke of,

The Trade - Off

but I believe we should head back to camp. We have a good three to four hour walk. I will explain while we walk."

Tim Connor

"Truth hurts, not the search after, the running from"

J. Eyberg

The Trade - Off

Chapter Eleven

Juan led the way back into the forest, leaving the city behind them. He began, "When I spoke of 'we' earlier, I was speaking in generalities. Every decision that every Earth person makes ultimately has an impact on every other person - either directly or indirectly. If, for example, you fail to smile at or acknowledge a stranger who passes you by while walking in the city, you send a message to that person that he is a non-person. That you are too wrapped up in your world to notice him or pay attention to him. Let's suppose that this person now feels slighted and repeats your behavior with everyone he meets and all of those people do likewise. It won't take very long before your lack of a smile is spread across the globe."

"Juan, I think you are getting a little carried away here. My lack of acknowledgment to a stranger in my building is not going to have that significant an impact worldwide. I will agree it might impact the person, but I can't buy that it will spread across the globe."

"Jason, there is a human consciousness that is bigger than you can ever begin to contemplate. And we don't have time now to go into further detail. We will have to save that discussion for your next trip when you bring your wife."

"Juan, although I am enjoying this little adventure, I don't plan to return again."

"You will be back again Jason, believe me."

The two continued in silence for the better part of two hours -Jason, with his thoughts, and Juan, with his plans. Juan suggested that they rest for a short time before they finished the last half of the trip back to the camp. Jason was troubled. He now understood the importance of decisions, choices and consequences - but there was something missing. He just couldn't put his mind on it. Juan interrupted Jason's thoughts, "Jason, it is now time for you to understand the second part of the message on the stone tablet - The Ten Life Actions. Let me give them to you briefly and we can then discuss any you question.

The Trade - Off

The Ten Life Actions are self-explanatory and do not require the degree of explanation that The Principles did."

"Juan, may I ask you a personal question?"

"Certainly."

"You have lived most of your life here in a remote village in southern Mexico where there are no schools, libraries, or computers. How have you become so educated? You speak eloquent English. You have a tremendous ability to discuss a wide variety of subjects, and your ability to communicate complicated concepts in a user-friendly way is astonishing. How have you learned all this here?"

"Jason, you flatter me. I am a humble and uneducated man. I do have the ability to think, reason and contemplate, but I would not say that I could ever successfully debate you or even one of your children on any everyday subject. I do thank you for the compliment.

"Before I share the *Ten Life Actions* with you, you need to understand that these are the companions to the Principles. One without the other renders either set useless. You see, Jason, to have the Ten Principles as your guide is a wonderful thing, but to not put them into action every day is to waste your awareness of them. For example, what good is it to let your wisdom give you understanding if you do nothing with either the wisdom or the understanding? What profit could you gain if, with gratitude, you inherit all things, and at some time in your life, when you are feeling discouraged, you let your discouragement completely fill your mind and influence your behavior. You would not be putting the Principle into action. Therefore, it is necessary to give a guide to correct actions that enables one to live within the framework of the Principles. Here are the Ten Life Actions."

- Ten Life Actions -

1. *If you cannot speak the truth, do not speak.*

2. *Commit to results once you have chosen.*

3. *Keep your life free of emotional clutter and stuff.*

4. *Be a student of life - not just an observer.*

5. *Treat everyone and everything with respect.*

6. *Remain true to what you believe and who you are.*

7. *Be a servant - not a master - in all things.*

8. *Live with a forgiving heart.*

9. *Every day thank God for all of your gifts.*

10. *Love everything and everyone without exception.*

Tim Connor

"Things don't change, we change."

Thoreau

The Trade - Off

Chapter Twelve

Juan quoted the Ten Life Actions as they continued their journey back to the camp. After stating all ten, he stopped in the narrow path and turned to face Jason. It was late in the afternoon and the sun was coming over Juan's left shoulder, beaming its way through the trees.

"Jason, please describe what your life looks like in twenty-five years."

"That's impossible Juan. No one can see the future. We have already discussed this in great detail."

"You miss the point. We create our future one day at a time with the decisions we make. Let's pretend you could create the ideal future for Jason Conroy. What does it look like?"

"I am healthy, happy and financially secure."

"A little more detail please."

"Why? Those four words say it all."

"Not quite. Let me give you an example. You could be happy - but alone. Healthy - but broken in spirit. Financially secure - but mentally weak. See what I mean?"

"No, Juan, I don't."

"OK Jason, we will play it your way for the time being. Let's assume you are fifty-five years old. Please answer the following questions.

"Are you working or retired?"

"Working."

"What are you doing for a career?"

"Self-employed."

"Doing what?"

"Consulting."

"How many hours a day or week?"

"Four hours a day, 25 hours a week."

"What else are you doing with the rest of your time?"

"Playing with my kids."

The Trade - Off

"No Jason, they will be on their own by then."

"Playing then."

"Playing what?"

"Juan, I don't know. These questions are stupid."

"Are they really? Jason, please humor me a just a little while longer. Playing what?"

"Golf."

"Every day?"

"Yes."

"Alone or with friends or your wife?"

"Both."

"Let's try another approach. Are you married?"

"Yes."

"To whom?"

"Cin, of course."

"Is she happy?"

"Yes."

"Are you sure?"

"Yes. You said I could create any circumstances I wanted."

"Are you happy?"

"Yes."

"Why?"

"Because I am doing what I want, in my career, relationships and other interests."

"Now to the crux of this entire issue. Let's take your marriage. If you continue to make decisions and actions as you have in the past in your relationship with your wife - will the outcome you say you want be a reality?"

"Good question, I am not sure."

"Do you have many friends, really good friends?"

"No, I have been too busy working all of these years to cultivate personal relationships."

"Then who are these people you will be playing golf with? Will they suddenly appear out of thin air?"

Jason didn't get a chance to answer because Juan quickened his pace as they entered the camp. Jason saw an elderly woman with two children. The children excitedly raced toward Juan and jumped into

The Trade - Off

his outstretched arms simultaneously. As Jason joined them, Juan introduced him to his two grandchildren - Vero and Hector. "Say hello to Mr. Conroy, children."

"Buenos Dios senor," they said in unison.

"Hello."

"Jason, this is my wife, Senora Anna Lopez. She does not speak any English."

She nodded and smiled at Jason as he returned the gesture.

"Please excuse me for a few moments while I catch up with the children. Why don't you settle in at the hut and think more about how you would like your life to turn out. We will continue our discussion after dinner. Anna will prepare an evening meal for all of us."

Jason headed for the hut and lay down on the cot to think about what Juan had asked him. It certainly had been a busy twenty-four hours. His head was spinning as he unsuccessfully fought off sleep. He quickly drifted off into a deep sleep. He was awakened a few hours later by Juan who said the meal was ready. Jason threw some cold water over his face and left the hut. While he was walking toward a small building that served as the dining area he realized that this was the first time in years he had had a peaceful sleep. No dreams. No nightmares. Just restful, quiet sleep. He woke refreshed and as hungry as any two people.

The dinner conversation between Juan, Jason and the children was jovial. Juan's grandchildren had that same sparkle that Juan had when he smiled. After dinner the children and Anna piled into their rickety old jeep and drove off.

"Juan, the children certainly are full of life. Where is their mother?"

"A few years ago while traveling in the United States with her husband on vacation, my daughter and son-in-law were gunned down in a small Texas town while shopping. The store was being robbed and they just happened to be in the wrong place at the wrong time. They got caught in some crossfire between the police and robbers. If they had chosen to take the longer route to the store that day rather than a shortcut, they would have arrived well after the police incident and would be alive today. Anna & I have raised the children ever since."

"I am so sorry. Do the children miss their parents? They look so happy."

"Don't be foolish Jason. Of course they miss them; they have just learned to live life in spite of their drama. Which I might add is what many people fail to do. Jason, life is not fair. It is not unfair either. Life doesn't pick on some people and leave others alone. It doesn't bestow gifts on a certain few and require others to live in poverty. We are all living with the consequences of our choices and actions. I have taught the children that in spite of their loss and grief, their life must go on. There is nothing any of us can do to bring their parents back. I would gladly trade my life for that of my daughter if I thought I could, but we all must continue to live each day and enjoy the gift of life that we have been given. Our purpose, their purpose and resolve must only be strengthened as a result of their tragedy. Let's rekindle the fire and pick up where we left off. So my friend, how do you want your life to turn out in the future?"

"I have given it some thought, but I must say, Juan, I don't know how to get more specific. And besides, I am not sure I want to. Won't getting too specific about my future twenty years from now limit my opportunities and options?"

"We will see. Jason, why don't you list those areas in your life that you believe are important."

"Well, let's see. There is my financial life, my relationships with my wife and children, my physical health and well being. Also, my mental development. And yes, my spiritual life. And social life. And my career or business."

"Lets take each of them one at a time and let's see if you can come up with one, just one, descriptive factor that you would like to see in the future. Let's start with your marriage."

"I would like to have a loving, respectful, supportive, nurturing and passionate relationship with Cin."

"What do you need to do now to ensure that that is what your marriage is like in twenty years?"

"I need to work at all of the aspects I described."

The Trade - Off

"What about your financial life?"

"I would like to be financially secure. Working only because I want to - not because I have to. And maintain my current standard of living."

"What do you need to do now to ensure that is what your financial life is like in twenty years?"

"I will need to work at all aspects of my financial life: earning, saving, spending wisely, and investing carefully."

"What about your spiritual life?"

"Got me there Juan."

"Let's come back to that one."

"What about your social life?"

"I would like to have a small group of good male and female friends as well as a number of good acquaintances."

"What do you need to do now to ensure this will be the case in twenty years?"

"I will need to work at developing relationships better."

"What about your physical life and health?"

"I would like to have the ability, energy and health to live an active life as long as I am alive."

"What do you need to do to ensure that this will be the case in twenty years?"

"I need to eat right, exercise more, get plenty of rest and manage the stress in my life."

"What about your mental development?"

"I would like to be able to develop and maintain new interests in music, art, literature and the theater."

"And next, what about your career and business?"

"I would like to work fewer days each month and maintain my income level. I would like to build the business and have the opportunity to offer it to my son one day if he is interested."

"What do you need to do to ensure that this will be the case in twenty years?"

"I need to work smarter, more creatively and network with people who can help me."

"And finally, your spiritual life?"

"Juan, for the life of me I don't know where to begin."

The Trade - Off

"That is one of your problems, Jason - one that must be addressed before you can leave."

Tim Connor

"You must begin to think of yourself as becoming the person you want to be."

David Viscott

Chapter Thirteen

"Jason, man is a spiritual being. His spirit and soul are temporarily housed in the physical body he is given at birth. When his body dies due to any number of causes, his spirit lives on. Every religion, believes in some form of spiritual life after physical death. Man wants to believe that there is something more to life than the seventy-odd years he is given here on Earth. Without getting into a deep debate about the benefit of religion, let's look at one of the common denominators in all of them. One thread you will see that is woven in all religions is the concept of consequences. Now it is generally believed that consequences come as a result of something that came before it. Would you agree?"

"So far."

"If consequences are a normal part of the life experience, what does man do to create consequences?"

"He decides and acts."

"What about the larger picture where one man, say a despot, decides and acts and starts a war, and as a result thousands die in combat. How did the individual decisions of each man or woman who died in combat bring them to the battlefield where they died? Or in other words, did the decision of one render meaningless the countless hundreds of decisions made by each person who was killed?"

"I can't answer that Juan."

"Let me see if I can help you understand, because this is one of the foundations of the spiritual aspect of life - that we are not alone but all connected in some spiritual or universal way. Let me give you an example from a painful period in my life that may shed some light on this issue for you.

"When my daughter was killed a few years ago, I found myself experiencing a wide variety of emotions: guilt, anger, grief, remorse, sadness and relief."

"Relief, Juan?"

The Trade - Off

"Let me explain please. My daughter was a bright, beautiful and loving child. She had just turned thirteen when it happened. At first we didn't notice. We thought she was just going through the normal physical changes from adolescence to her teenage years. So we did nothing. Then, as her condition worsened, we knew it was more serious. When we took her to Mexico City to a hospital, we discovered she had a rare incurable disease and had only a few years to live. Later, when she visited Texas, she had outlived all of the medical profession's predictions by several years and she appeared to be doing fine. But we all knew deep inside that one day this horrible disease would end her life; we just didn't know when. She was like a time bomb ticking down one second at a time, but no one knew what the time was when it began its countdown - so we didn't know how much time she had left. When her children were born, we were concerned for their health, but they have shown no sign of her condition – which, by the way, is hereditary and passed from one generation to the next. When we were notified of her death, my relief came because I knew her ending from the disease would be long, painful and humiliating. This event prevented her - no all of us

- from having to undergo that dreadful experience. We can now remember her as she was, a vibrant, pretty, and loving daughter and mother.

There is more, but I want you to know that her death was a turning point in my spiritual life. I had always believed that the spiritual dimension was for those special people: the Gurus, Monks, Priests and Healers. But as time passed, I learned that each of us must confront our own life from a direction other than the physical side where we can only see reality. Spirituality does not deal in reality, but with the less visible side of life. My anger came from the fact that I was unable to prevent her dying in a foreign country amongst strangers. The source of my grief was that I left unsaid many things to her while she was alive, and now I can only communicate these to her in my prayers."

"I am so sorry Juan. That must have been a painful time for you and your wife."

The Trade - Off

"There is more. Her mother died months later of a broken heart. She just could no longer deal with the pain and sadness."

"You have had a difficult journey."

"Jason, you are quite right but that journey led to my current mental state of peace in my consciousness. First there must be pain - and then peace. First anger - then acceptance. First denial - then positive change."

"Why have you chosen to share this story with me now?"

"You must realize, Jason, that all growth sooner or later comes from incorrect decisions and actions, struggle and the awareness that something must change in your life. There is no other way. You learn nothing when you make right decisions or choices."

"But I have not had what I would call a difficult life."

"That is my point. You will create a life of struggle, frustration and disappointment if you fail to recognize your spiritual nature and the lessons it can teach you as you grow in maturity and wisdom. So, my friend, what is your spiritual nature or Soul trying to teach you now?"

"I am not sure."

Tim Connor

"I have to go to the village to pick up a few supplies. Why don't you spend some time in quiet contemplation considering the spiritual aspect of decisions and choices? We will complete our discussion when I return."

The Trade - Off

"If you are strong enough, there are no precedents."

F. Scott Fitzgerald

Chapter Fourteen

As Juan drove off in darkness, Jason watched the taillights become a faint glow, then blackness. Jason returned to his temporary home away from home, lit a lantern, and sat and considered his life. In general, it had been good. His childhood was fairly typical. He grew up in a small mid-western town with what he felt were reasonably normal parents. They did not have an affluent lifestyle, but he never wanted for anything that was important. His career was more successful than most, but he felt that was due in part to his dedication, commitment, and time that he devoted to his work. He had made more money in a year than his father had in his entire career. His relationships were as good as could be expected given the other demands on his life.

The Trade - Off

So where's the problem? he thought. Could any of them be better? Could he have it all, or at least more than he had experienced and accumulated so far? The answer crept up on him from the far recesses of his mind. Yes, you can learn more, have more, accomplish more, share more and be more. But, you can't do it until you let go of your emotional and psychological need for these and turn over the satisfaction of your expectations to your spiritual side.

"How do I do this?" he said half out loud.

"You release the expected and embrace the unexpected," his inner voice answered.

"Wow, I am having a conversation with myself. This is a strange new experience."

"This is not a new experience Jason. We have been trying to get you to pay attention for years, but you had too much noise and clutter in your life to listen."

"OK, I admit I have been busy, but it was necessary to accomplish my needs and desires."

"Can you imagine how much more you might have achieved had you been willing to let us help?"

"Who is us?"

"It is the experience of all who have come before you. It is the knowledge of the ages, all at your disposal if you would have been willing to tune us in and not turn us off."

"OK, I am listening now. What do you want me to know?"

"You have come to this remote village for a purpose. Juan is your guide. Listen to his wisdom and the lessons of the *Ten Life Principles* and *Ten Life Actions*. They will guide your journey and ensure a happy, productive, peaceful and successful life."

"Is that all?'

There was no answer. Jason waited. But the conversation with himself, or whomever he was talking with, was apparently over. He decided to review the Ten Life Principles and Ten Life Actions. He decided to evaluate where he was the weakest so that he could begin to make some positive changes. He came to the conclusion, after careful thought, that he needed the most work on numbers three,

The Trade-Off

four, nine and ten of The Principles and numbers three, four, seven and nine of the Ten Life Actions. Now the real work must begin.

Juan had not yet returned from his trip to the village, so Jason decided to map out a strategy to ensure that once he returned home his trip here would not have been in vain. He began to write down some objectives and possible obstacles to his success in the areas he had decided needed the most immediate work. It was past midnight before Juan returned with a few staples and some food.

"What have you been up to these past few hours, Jason?"

Jason spent the next hour explaining the conclusions he had come to while he was alone. He left out the part of the conversation with himself - for whatever reason.

"So, my friend, what is your next step?"
"I will leave for home in the morning and put into place my plan."

"Not so fast. Everyone at one time or another has good intentions. Most people, however, never follow through with their intentions. They usually let something or someone get in their way. This was Frank's problem as well, and it took us several months for him to learn to take back control of his life."

"Juan, I don't have several months."

"Jason, neither do I. I have recently discovered that I have the same disease as my daughter and my time with you is coming to an end."

When Jason woke the next morning, Juan was gone. He left no note or any reason for his departure or explanation if he would be back. Jason waited until mid-afternoon and then decided to begin his journey home.

The Trade - Off

"We are what we think. All that we are arises with our thoughts. With our thoughts we make our world."

The Buddha

- Epilogue -

Jason felt a gentle nudge that brought him back to active consciousness. He slowly opened his eyes and saw the smiling face of his mother looking down on him with love. "Wake up sleepy head or you will be late for school. You don't want to miss your last day of high school and the opportunity to say good-bye to friends, some of whom you may never see again."

"Mom, what's the date today?"

"Why son?"

"Please, just tell me the date."

"It is May 19th."

"It can't be."

"Jason, what is wrong?"

"Mom, have I been asleep for more than one night?"

"Jason, you are kidding aren't you?"

The Trade - Off

"Mom, I have never been more serious."

"No, just one normal night's sleep."

"It was anything but normal. I must have been dreaming, but it seemed so real. I just don't know. It is too complicated to explain now. Later, OK?"

"OK, but you better get dressed and ready for school or you will be late for your last day."

When Jason had finished dressing and was tying his shoes, he bent down, and as he did his keys fell from his back pocket. As he reached down to pick them up he noticed a small piece of paper - the edge sticking out from under his bedspread where it neatly touched the floor. He pulled the paper out from under the bed and read the short paragraph. His face turned snow white. He couldn't believe his eyes.

"It isn't possible," he said, half out loud. "It just can't be true."

But he couldn't deny its existence. He was holding in his shaking hands a small section of paper that was obviously a torn piece from a larger piece of paper. It was a yellowish brown color and the print was barely visible. He slowly read, *"Principle Number Two............"*, but he just couldn't finish it.

He sat on the end of his bed in shock and could only repeat the same words over and over again, "how, why?"

He put the paper in his pocket went down to breakfast after some of the color had returned to his face. He said goodbye to his mother and left for school. As he was pulling into the school parking lot, he noticed a man running toward the spot where he was going to park. Jason parked the car, got out and the man just stopped a few feet from him and stood watching him, staring at him.

"Is there something you want?" Jason asked.

The Trade - Off

The man came even closer, smiled and handed Jason an envelope. But before he turned away he said, "I have been trying to give this to you for several months but you kept running from me." He then turned and slowly walked away. Inside were two sheets of paper. The first was a note. Jason read it slowly as disbelief took over his mind.

"Twice in one morning. What is going on?" He read the note slowly.

"*Jason,*

Always remember I am with you in all of your triumphs as well as your trials. All of your victories and all of your failures. All of your mistakes as well as all of your lessons. The choices you make will forever impact your future, so chose wisely, my friend using your understanding of the Ten Life Principles as the foundation for each and every decision you make. I have enclosed a parting gift for you.

Tim Connor

Keep it with you at all times and honor its wisdom - and you cannot fail to build a life worth living."

I will see you again soon Jason - in your dreams!

Juan

Jason looked back to see if he could see the man who had given him the envelope, but he was gone. He just vanished into thin air. Then he pulled the second piece of paper out of the envelope and read the first line on the top of the page: **The Ten Life Principles**. There was a short paragraph under each Principle. Except for Number Two, which was blank on the page. It was odd because the paper wasn't torn; it was a perfect piece of eight and one-half by eleven stationery.

There were shadow lines, however, where Principle Number Two must have been at one time. He pulled out the piece of torn paper from his pocket and stretched it out directly under the First Principle. It was a perfect match. The shadow lines on the bigger

The Trade - Off

piece fit perfectly with the torn edges of his piece. The color of both pieces was perfectly matched. Jason felt a unique combination of fear and excitement. What did all of this mean? Was his dream last night a dream or was his experience somehow miraculously real?

As he was considering its meaning and implications, he heard Marjorie's voice from across the parking lot as she was jogging toward him, "Jason, are you coming to school or are you going to spend all day baby-sitting your car?"

As she got close enough to him to see his expression, she asked, "Are you OK? You look as if you have seen a ghost."

"I'll be fine. Thanks Margie. It is too complicated to explain now. I'll tell you later this summer when we have more time."

And then he just hugged her and held on for what seemed like several minutes and whispered in her ear, "Marjorie, I love you. You take care of yourself while you are at Harvard."

Tim Connor

"I will, don't worry Jason."

"No, I mean it. You be careful."

Together, arm in arm, Jason and Marjorie walked into school for the very last time, each with different thoughts filling their minds about what the future might bring…

The Trade - Off

"Keep your face to the sunshine and you cannot see the shadows."

Helen Keller

Titles available from: Connor *Resource* Group

Mail orders: Tim Connor, CSP, Connor Resource Group, Box 397, Davidson, NC 28036 USA
Tel. Orders: (800) 222-9070 • (704) 895-1230 • Fax Orders: (800) 222-9071 • E-Mail: speaker@bellsouth.net
Website: www.timconnor.com

BOOKS AND MANUALS	Price	Qty	Size	Amount
The Trade-Off	15.00			
Sales Mastery	24.95			
Life Balance Newsletter (12 issues)	96.00			
Soft Sell (paperback)	12.95			
52 Network Marketing Tips	8.95			
Daily Success Journal	45.00			
Success Journal (30 day trial version)	7.50			
The Voyage	15.00			
The Road to Happiness is Full of Potholes	11.95			
The Road to Happiness Fun Book	5.95			
Win-Win Selling	19.95			
The Ancient Scrolls	15.00			
Success Book Club	$85.00			
Tim's weekly E-Mail Tips	25.00 Topic/ YR			
(Mgt., Sales, Motivation, Relationships, Success) Topic/ YR				

AUDIO CASSETTES	Price	Qty	Size	Amount
Soft Sell Sales Courses	195.00			
Sales Development Skills	70.00			
Personal Development Skills	70.00			
Management Development Skills	70.00			
The Road to Happiness Audio Series	20.00			
Master Speakers Int'l Beating Your Competition	85.00			
Soft Sell Mini Cassette Album	25.00			
Search (8 cassettes)	85.00			

PAYMENT METHOD

☐ Enclosed is my check for $_____
☐ Charge my: VISA/MC/Amex/Discover
$_____
No: _____
Exp. Date: _____
Signature: _____

SUBTOTAL $_____
(ADD SHIPPING) $_____5.00
Prices are quoted in US Funds
TOTAL $_____

TO ORDER - Please Print Clearly

Name: _____
Tel No. _____
Org.: _____ Position: _____
Address: _____
City: _____ State: _____ Country: _____ Zip: _____

☐ Please send information on Tim's services as a keynote speaker, trainer and/or consultant.